Tom Crowley faces challenges with scheduling

The morning of Bring Your Daughter to Work Day began for me in silence. The hall sagged with the outlines of our coats, the family coats on the family coat rack, blocking the light from the front door.

This sight always depressed me a little bit, like surely we could have more light in the place? And I ought to have done something about it, but then, what if it was a cold day? Everyone would get cold. I hated to think of everyone either cold because I had moved their coats, or cross because they were late because they had to find their coats. Or if it rained! All of them soaked and it would be my fault. So the coats were there, swallowing the light, unwanted guests who would never come in.

The kitchen was trashed. Looking now like a kind of recreation of an abandoned wartime home you might see in a museum. Like everyone had fled to the bunker and left all their crap everywhere. There were plates and half-mugs of cold tea. There was the classic strand of hair on the butter, on the knife, on the chopping board.

My family, they had evacuated, it seemed, and left me behind. I was also probably late. A panic swept in – that's what an empty kitchen can do to me. I moved dirty crockery around without quite seeing how I could organise it into the dishwasher. A stack of pans from the night before was still on the hob, needing to be washed. I moved a frying pan to the sink and back again. I boiled the kettle and forgot about it until the water was too cool to use. I wished there was someone there to talk to. I was tired, is what I'm saying. I don't know why I'm saying it. But I'm saying it. Normally things – or not normally – but things have, in the past, felt less out of my control. Like, I do actually know how to stay on top of domestic work. I do know. But on that day, I felt alone. The whole day was at the wrong angle somehow.

My son, whose loudness and colour would normally have been present, had gone out early for badminton practice before school. He'd learnt not to wake me in the mornings because I always asked awkward questions about his routine. Why he hadn't put the lid back on the toothpaste, or why he'd left the wardrobe door hanging open in his bedroom, and the light on, and his bed unmade again, and what's this all over your school-work? I never seemed to stop. He didn't want the hassle of me first thing in the morning and I couldn't blame him. Poor kid. Do you know, I used to have to go after him when we argued? I'd pursue him along the morning street, hold him back from his march to the bus stop, press his small dinosaur-ish head close to my chest and tell him I was sorry, that I loved him. 'Dad, you've got no shoes on,' he'd say. He'd give me his sad look and turn away for school, and I would walk back down the street, avoiding glass, feeling ashamed and temporarily heartbroken. I'd get through the door, text him again to say sorry for being silly, and how proud I am and then my daughter would be there, and time to make more breakfast and go through the whole routine again.

The Expansion Project

Ben Pester

GRANTA

Granta Publications, 12 Addison Avenue, London W11 4QR
First published in Great Britain by Granta Books, 2025

A CIP catalogue record for this book is available from the British Library.

1 3 5 7 9 10 8 6 4 2

ISBN 978 1 80351 258 7
eISBN 978 1 80351 259 4

Typeset in Adobe Garamond by Iram Allam

Printed and bound by CPI Group (UK) Ltd, Croydon, CR0 4YY

The manufacturer's authorised representative in the EU
for product safety is Authorised Rep Compliance Ltd,
71 Lower Baggot Street, Dublin D02 P593, Ireland.
www.arccompliance.com

www.granta.com

For Emilie, Orson and Coco

Contents

So he was out at badminton club. Eliane too, she was gone. An appointment with a client – before getting up, I had vaguely heard her getting her things ready, packing her camera, her suitcase of colour swatches, her anger at the measuring tape that was lost again.

Many times since I have told myself, I could have got up early that morning, I should have got the place clean and made her a cup of tea. Normally I would have. Normally we would've discussed how things were going to play out, checked I had the right day. I can actually hear her asking me, Is that definitely today? Bring Your Daughter to Work Day? Is that definitely today?

I would then have seen my son too, asked him about badminton, checked the colour of his teeth, smelled his breath. I could have settled on the morning, made better decisions. Ruffled his hair, told him I loved him, that he was doing everything just fine.

But that time had gone – the shapes of their morning marked by egg stains and cold dregs of tea were all I was left with. I was wearing my most dismal pyjamas, looking at the mess, feeling beaten by the day already when her voice jerked me back to life.

'Hey Daddy!'

My daughter was in the doorway, already dressed. She was, as instructed, dressed in dungarees and – a jumper – I don't recall which jumper. I wish I could remember exactly what she was wearing. It would have been better if I'd remembered these things. Or maybe it wouldn't have made any difference. Anyway – she was there and she was dressed like someone who was definitely not going to school.

'Ah hello. I suppose you're coming to work with me then, are you?' I said.

'Yep.'

'And are you going to actually do any work?'

'OK. Er what do I have to do?'

'We have to write messaging.'

'Messages? I have to write messages?'

'Yeah, sort of. You have to write little messages to help people feel good about their work. Like "we succeed together", or something like that.'

She looked thoughtful for a minute. I asked if she had an idea for a message. She nodded.

'Go on then. Tell me your message on this dark morning.'

She took a breath and said, in a strange voice:

'"In the darkness, we grow, we succeed together, we love and break together. I am so sorry."'

'Ha, wow. I love it, Hen! What was that bit about being sorry?'

'I don't know.'

'And the darkness?'

A shrug, nothing more. We moved on. We chatted about how she had slept, whether she had seen her mum or her brother before they left, and if they were OK, and we hugged several times until finally I set her at the breakfast counter and poured out her cereal. She looked at it for a while and made a face.

'I'm not hungry yet,' she said.

'Yet? What's yet? Not hungry yet?'

'I'm not hungry for this.' She nudged the cereal away from her.

'Please,' I said. 'Eat a bit or we won't be able to go.'

'I want to save space,' she said.

'Save space? What for?'

'You said we would get croissants at the station.'

The croissant at the station was not meant to be the full breakfast. It was clearly designated as a treat, rather than a meal. I felt the stress of the day unrolling in front of me. A premonition of anger. Do you know about this anger? When you can feel angry for a child being and behaving in the exact way a human child is supposed to behave, unreasonableness and stress start bubbling because, for example, your eight-year-old daughter is prioritising her food intake in a way that would be normal for any adult.

My parents were terrible for this. I remember the stone I would have in my stomach whenever it was dinner time, and the food was way too salty, or just seemed to be endless, and my father would watch us, on the edge of losing it because me or my brother or my sister could not eat the food.

There are children, he would say. In this world, there are children living like animals. And it was true, but of course there also were many of us who were not starving, but were slowly being traumatised by our parents and their anger. They seemed not to be themselves at those times, those heavy people. You told me you wanted this! they'd yell. This was your idea! I tried not to hear them, or see the spit on the corner of their mouths. Redness on their necks, heavy heavy steam from the kettle over and over again being boiled but no drink made. I rifled through the spoons and thought about the day ahead.

Our irrational anger comes from our own parents being angry with us. I heard that somewhere, or I read it. Where did I read it? I don't know. It will have been something on my phone. On the toilet. Trying to reassure myself that things are OK. In fact, it is trauma, and we carry it around. We are unaware of it until we are in proximity with a child we are responsible for, and there it is, suddenly a whole library of delicately formed intolerances. Loudness is a common trigger. As though a child knows what volume is correct in the adult world. Food is another. Some adults find greed insufferable, or loud eating noises, or pickiness. Or slowness. All these crazy ignitions, like fragile bottles of perfume that will fall from their narrow ledge and shatter at the slightest disruption.

Sometimes I would remember this and force myself not to explode over the wasted food. I had all sorts of techniques and reminders and coping mechanisms, but if we were late, and the house was already a mess, if she was being argumentative, these things caused me to almost completely shut down.

'Do you promise to eat the croissant then?' I said.

'Of course I do!'

'You promise to eat the whole croissant and not make a mess?'

She made this impossible promise, and I ate her cereal. As I ate the soft flakes of bran, or whatever this was meant to be, I tried not to go on about food waste.

'You'll need something else though,' I said. 'Not just a croissant at the station.'

'Chocolate spread on toast?'

'No, something healthy.'

I persuaded her to eat a banana, and we had some relief there. I told her I loved her because of her willingness to eat a banana. While she ate, we did the list.

'Teeth clean?'

'Not yet, obviously.'

'Dressed?'

'Yes. Daddy, look, you can see me.'

'Face washed and monster-ised?'

'Moisturised, Daddy. Yep.'

'Bag with your drawing stuff and a book?'

'Yes, and Picolo.'

'Who's Picolo? Actually I think I know, don't open your bag. Finish your banana.'

'OK, Picolo is the pink and green unicorn cat.'

'I thought so. I know Picolo, of course I do.'

There were about five of her cuddly toys that this could have been. They mattered a great deal, but their names were new every day, it seemed. They had enormous eyes, and when they were arranged in a row they had the impact of a ghoulish planetary takeover. They were very similar to the ones that seemed to be advertised everywhere, but she would get hers in strange places. Picolo was found in a park at dusk. There was nobody else to claim it. The idea of leaving it to be found in the morning drew instant ragged tears from my daughter. Not because she wanted the toy, but because she couldn't stand the idea of leaving it out all night by itself. We agreed to leave a note about Picolo. I wrote down what she instructed, that anyone who had lost a cat unicorn could go to the school and ask for Hen.

We left the note under a rock on the bench. It was gone when we walked past the next morning, and Picolo, via the very mildest possible washing machine cycle, was added to the family.

'Hair?'

'Yep.'

'No Hen – look, your hair is not done. Get me the hairbrush, I'll do it.'

She shouted and grimaced while I brushed her hair, as she always did. I can't be specific about what I would have said at that time, but this shouting over the hair-brushing was another potential trigger for the day to fall apart. I'm making myself sound like a bad parent. You should know that I am talking about experiences that happen far below the surface. I always made sure my kids were happy and safe and well fed and had a future ahead of them. I'm just, now, for whatever reason, just being honest. Just very honest. I'm saying all this. Whatever this is. Whatever I'm doing here, honestly.

I would have said something about knowing it's not fair that her hair got dashed and tangled like that, and how sorry I was, how gentle I was trying to be, hundreds of times, little repeated noises. I would have said, this is only the start of the day, there is so much more of the day to get through, can you please just hold still while I brush your hair. I would have said a thousand things, or it felt like it, because hearing her scream and cry each morning when I had to brush her hair was, in itself, an endless period of time, which I had to fill with soothing noises.

It was a space that continues now, if I think about it, one of many rooms that seem to have appeared, or if not rooms, then buildings, in which I am there trying to calm and soothe and make happy and amuse my daughter, in which there is nothing but her and me, and the sounds we make to communicate to each other, this is OK, we're doing OK.

My children, since they were born, have been a miraculous way for me to confirm that I am all right. I certainly couldn't have said it before they arrived. I was not all right.

I might as well be honest and say I was never good at my job. Until it was for them, I never had a single second at work that felt like a productive use of my time. Not here, not in any of my jobs before this one.

I'm good at my job, of course, and I have deadened those urges to run away that were so keen when I was younger, when even the smell of an office was the first sensation of feeling myself fade away.

Soon enough, with the house an even more dismal mess than when I'd got up, we were ready.

We stepped out into the street and saw nobody at all. I could hear cars, but it was a slow morning. There were no faces at the windows of the street. Not even Chucky, the toddler across the road, who would press his face against the glass and stare into our house, sometimes audibly growling.

Geese flew over the houses on our terraced street, honking to each other.

'Those your friends?' I asked Hen.

'No!'

'Hen! Your friends just went past!'

'I don't even know what you're talking about.' She was laughing. It filled the whole street.

'Onk onk onk.' I chased her up the road. 'Onk onk onk!'

We reached the bus stop just in time to get the 29 to the station.

'Are you going to behave yourself today?' I asked.

'Yes Daddy, of course.'

It annoyed her to be asked this all the time. I knew that it was pretty much the worst question I could ask her, but something was off. Something was not balanced – it occurred to me that I should have insisted she ate the cereal before we left. She was hungry, and the bus was now moving slowly. Even though we had plenty of time, I felt sure it had been too long since she got up and she had not enough food to keep her blood sugar at the right levels for the day ahead.

'Are you looking forward to it?'

'So much! Can we eat in the café at your work?'

'The canteen, yes. Yes, I think we will.'

We got to the station in good time. The croissant score was good – flaky, warm, large. I bought myself a coffee and a sausage roll for the journey. The train was delayed by eight minutes. We waited in the cold. I tried to keep her still, tried to get her to eat her croissant, but she wanted to wait until we got on the train.

'You're always trying to get me to do things,' she said. It was true.

Nearby, I heard a couple having quite a heated debate. They were discussing a third person, it sounded like. I only got a few snatches of what they were saying, but somehow the whole conversation seemed to make perfect sense to me. They were concerned about someone they both knew. A flatmate possibly?

'He's going to lose that job,' one of them was saying. 'He keeps calling in sick. He doesn't give a shit. And he never washes. I can feel it, he's gonna lose the job and it will come back to us.'

Yes, a flatmate, I remember thinking. It sounded like they were annoyed that their flatmate was going to lose his job. I felt sure of it. The world settled on this knowledge for a moment.

'Don't worry,' the other one said. 'He's pretty much indispensable, your brother. They won't sack him.'

'You always tell me not to worry, but you won't say that when my mother is in our house because he can't afford to keep her!'

Ah, so a brother, then? They were discussing a brother. And the brother looks after the mother. The mother is sick.

'Your mother is welcome whenever she needs to come here,' the man was saying. He sounded like an idiot. Disconnected. I took against him immediately.

After a few seconds of silence, the woman looked in my direction. She had caught me pretty obviously staring at her and her partner, who I now hated. I smiled. She smiled briefly, a moment of genuine warmth, and then looked away. I turned my attention back to Hen. But Hen was not where I last saw her. This was classic.

'Hen, please come back and sit down,' I called.

She had gone to the furthest end of the platform, where it sloped down into the tracks.

I felt a surging alarm that she had got so far away. She looked tiny. A train was coming, not due to stop there, moving fast.

'Hen!' I called again. The train was getting closer, but of course she was not actually anywhere near the edge of the platform. The train would not collide with her, but the size and volume of it all made me dizzy.

I could feel the eyes of the couple looking at me. I forced myself to see the funny side. To speak in the gentle parenting voice that seemed to be the only acceptable way now in public.

'Hen! Come on, please, I'm bored all by myself!'

She didn't hear me. She had her hands over her ears because the train was now shooting through, savaging the air of the station.

'Jesus!' said the man of the couple behind me. 'That can't be legal. Coming through at that speed.'

'Of course it's legal!' said the woman.

'Someone could get hurt,' the man said.

'Fucking hell will you ever stop saying the first thing that comes into your head?'

Soon I was too far away to hear them any more. Hen was shivering a little bit when I got to her. Her face was freezing cold. 'You need to stop wandering off,' I said.

'I didn't wander off.'

'You need to start listening to me.'

'I couldn't hear you because of the train! It really scared me, and now you're shouting.' She threatened to cry. She made that sound, a high groan that preceded tears sometimes, and other times brattishness.

'I'm not shouting,' I said loudly.

'Well, I'm not wandering off!'

I muttered fucksake under my breath. I looked away from Hen and back along the track to where the couple were standing sullenly. I looked at my phone – the train was due.

'Come on,' I said. 'Let's find a good spot to get on the train.'

The best spots were actually back down towards the front, but I didn't want to walk near the couple again. The man seemed to be glaring at me. I took a few steps and then stopped on the yellow line to wait for the train.

'We can't stop here,' Hen said.

'This is the best place,' I told her.

'But—'

I raised my voice again. 'No! Hen will you stand still and wait here for the train? Unbelievable the stress of this already!'

I heard Hen continuing to manoeuvre around me, felt her pulling on my arm, but I ignored it. I stood there and looked at the track going back away north.

I mean, I think it was north. Is it relevant?

My sense of direction is dreadful. I just looked into the distance, the white sky. The trees. I tried to see a bird and calm down. If there had been a bird, maybe I could have found some peace. There was no bird. There were no birds at all. I mean there was nothing. It was – I remember – it was a completely empty space, the sky. Just nothing. Hen was still irritating me.

I was just hungry, I told myself. I let the time pass, just looking at the sky. My stomach was churning, but I remembered at least there was a sausage roll. Even if there was no sign of life in the entire sky, there was still a sausage roll.

'Have you realised why we can't stand here yet, Daddy?'

Hen was grinning at me and looking back down the platform.

I looked back at our bench. All our stuff was still there. My coat, my bag, the croissant, my coffee, all of it was still there.

I wanted to rush back to it all. Not least because of the series of punishments that used to be in place for losing your work laptop. They would not actually take disciplinary action, but there was definitely a list or something you ended up on.

People on that list had to have additional security training and patronising workshops. My mental health would be called into question – and I would be assigned some kind of mindfulness app to make sure I was connected and grounded and in constant physical contact with the property of the company. Plus, I really wanted that sausage roll!

And yet, it was all just there. I dared myself to leave it.

'Aren't you going to get your stuff?' Hen asked.

'In a minute,' I said.

It seemed more important to find a sign of life. I looked back at the sky – surely there would be something. At this stage, an insect would've done. The meanest fly.

'What are you staring at?' Hen asked. There was a note of concern in her voice. I had been far too stressed with everything, I realised. Why was I always like this with her? Why was I like this with my whole family?

'Daddy, what are you staring at?'

'Nothing. I'm looking for your goose friends. Onk onk.'

She didn't respond. She pulled my hand again but I snapped my arm away. We glared at one another. Then smiled. Then, slowly, went back to looking at the sky, me glancing at the little pile of our stuff every couple of seconds.

'I can see a parakeet!' she said.

I looked where she was pointing. 'There's nothing there,' I said.

'Right there – two of them – woo! Beautiful!'

'Stop it,' I said. 'There's nothing there.'

'Look! Green and yellow – so fast! I can see four of them.'

'I mean it, stop being silly now.'

'I'm not! Look, can't you see?'

I looked again but the sky gave me nothing. Greenish white, the colour of the underside of a cabbage. Fucksake, I whispered, again, she heard me but had learnt long ago, or had it on instinct, that this expletive was not meant for her.

We had left it too long. The train was coming. I ran back and scrabbled for my work bag, picking up and dropping and then picking up again all the little accoutrements that had been gathered to make Hen happy. I bundled her onto the train and sighed.

After finding a place to sit, we realised that the napkins that had come with the croissants were not with us. They were on the bench along with my sausage roll.

'This is my fault, Hen. I'm so sorry.'

She nodded solemnly. 'It's OK.'

'OK, but your fingers! You're getting grease everywhere.'

Silence from her now. I wiped her fingers with my hands in between her pulling apart wedges of the croissant. I noticed that there were grease marks on her white jumper, her smart one, that was a gift from my wife Eliane's aunty. It was definitely ruined.

'I'll get some loo roll from the toilet,' I said. 'Give me the jumper too.'

I took her jumper and left her with my laptop and everything else. I got the idea that people were looking at me, but when I tried to meet their eyes, they turned away. I was aware that my face was red. I get blotchy with stress.

It's instant, this reddening: before the language of my anger has come, the body has its own expression. I cannot name or reason what's happening, but I change colour like a lizard, like a storm. The first toilet I came to was locked. I looked back, but could not see Hen.

'I'm looking further up the carriage, Hen. Hen!' She didn't hear me. A very punchable-looking man glared at me.

The next toilet was locked – the only other one on the train. We were approaching a stop. I had visions of Hen getting off the train because I wasn't there. Or of someone getting on – someone with my face, someone with my voice, hopping onto the train and grabbing her by the arm and dragging her away. I rushed back to our seats.

'The toilet is locked. And there's only one on the train,' I said. I handed back her jumper and told her to put it on.

'There's another one up there,' Hen said.

'No there isn't there is only one and someone is in it.'

The woman in the seat behind Hen looked up at me. I recognised her as a regular commuter. She knew I was lying and that there were more toilets on the train. Our eyes met for a second. She seemed to want to say something, so I stared harder. Sort of daring her to contradict me. She looked away – my only victory of the morning, and I wasn't proud of it.

'I really need a napkin, Daddy.'

'Yeah well, we left them behind. Maybe if you had been listening to me I wouldn't have left them.'

'You said it was your fault.'

'Well maybe it's your fault too. Jesus – look at the state of this, what happened?'

It must have been when I got up, but coffee had splashed everywhere across the table. Hen was moving it around with her fingers. She looked pleased with the shapes she was making.

'We really need napkins Daddy.'

I restarted the search through my bag. I felt sure there would be something. I'm forever storing napkins ahead of exactly this kind of event.

'It's OK,' I said, struggling to keep my breathing steady. 'It's just coffee. Look, don't use your hands, chicken, it's OK. I'm sure I've got something. Aha! Yes! Look!'

I had finally laid my hands on a grubby packet of tissues from the last time she'd had a cold.

'Daddy – what am I actually doing today?' Hen asked. I was wiping the table.

'I still need to check all that. If you can just sit and keep out of trouble for ten seconds, when I've finished cleaning up after you, I will look on my phone. Just stop messing about.'

'I haven't done anything!'

'All right. I know, but just sit calmly. Just read your book. Play with Picolo. Look out the window.'

'I am!'

'All right, all right. Sorry.'

I tried again to find details of the day, but there were other emails appearing, people chasing me for unfinished work, an invite to an important-sounding town hall meeting with important announcements; I tried to get my head straight. I started answering an email from my line manager.

'I need the toilet,' Hen said. It didn't seem possible that she could need to go now. It had only been an hour since she last went.

'You can't go. There's someone in there.'

'They might have finished.'

'They haven't finished, they haven't bought a ticket, so they won't come out of there until we arrive.'

'How do you know?'

'Because I just do. Sometimes you just need to hide in the toilet.'

There was silence as she looked at me. I could see her wondering if this was true, if there really was a man hiding in the toilet. I was almost holding my breath. I did not know why I wanted to tell her there was a man in the toilet, apart from that is what I assumed was happening. And as I sat there I realised that yes, of course, all of the toilets are full because people need to hide. Hen watched me thinking this, and then some switch went off and she quietly lost interest in the subject, but we both knew she would come back to it later.

'Can I have a drink?'

'You have a bottle of water.'

'I left it with the napkins.'

'What!?'

'I'm sorry, Daddy!'

'Jesus fucking Christ.' This I whispered, and Hen knew not to quite hear it but of course she did hear it.

'Can I have a drink then?'

'Where from? Where can I get you a drink now? There's nothing on the train.'

'Well I didn't know that, did I?'

'Look, just get it together,' I snapped eventually, hating the sound my voice was making in the quiet train. 'They won't let me bring you into the building if you keep this up! Just wait until we arrive, I will get you another bottle of water. Then we can go to the office and have a nice day OK? I am sorry for getting cross.'

She tried to get out of her seat, claiming again to need the toilet.

'Sit down for godssake.'

'He might have finished.'

I do not know why I felt the need to defend the man in the toilet, if he was even in there, but I felt urgently that he needed to be left alone, and Hen needed to understand to leave people alone when they are in the toilet.

'He hasn't. He isn't going to finish. He hides in there every day because he can't afford the train to work. Leave him alone.'

I held her arm, not tight, it didn't hurt her, but it was not nice. It was not how you'd like to see yourself holding your kid's arm.

'I need you to sit down now and be calm, OK?'

'I know, let go of me! Jeez!'

'Jeez? What's jeez?'

'Nothing. Just let go.'

I let go and felt the shame slide in where anger had snaked away. I put my phone away. Held her hand. Kissed her head. Wondered if anyone else from work was having this trouble today. Wondered if the people on the train were thinking about calling social services. Probably not. It was probably fine. I did a crossword clue on my phone. I tried to breathe more calmly.

Archivist's note

I have requested the style guide for this archive several times, and nothing has come through. It makes it very hard to know where the beginning is.

This, what you're reading now, just contains my casual notes. It is one of many threads I have been working on, and I don't even know if I have done this work correctly. I certainly think it's worthwhile, but my judgement is not the same as the judgement of the Capmeadow Ownership and Experience team. Which is who I think I work for.

What I am aiming for is just one way to understand the rich and productive history of the Capmeadow Expansion Project. There are many, many others. For example, there are several digital artefacts that allude to abandoned projects in which teams have tried to either commemorate (the great expansion centenary moment) or explain (the radical-thinking footage in which several colleagues appear to draw maps on their bodies as a way of defining the ever-changing scope of the Capmeadow estate) or justify (the remains of graffiti exclaiming The Expansion is a Disease!) the work that happens here.

I'll probably delete most of the content here, once I have the style guide.

Once I have the dates and linear order – without which it's impossible to know how long all of this has taken. When was any of this happening? How long ago? Until I have the style guide and linear record, I simply can't tell you.

I increasingly think the style guide and linear order referencing I have been repeatedly promised actually won't, and maybe can't, exist.

I will delete all of this, probably, as I have said. But first, let's see, let's try.

There are so many places that could be called a starting point, I get dizzy. It could be here, with this voice. Not *this* voice, not my voice. But the voice of the AV technician, which I am introducing now. This is the introduction. Or the placeholder for the introduction.

I feel sure that the archive has tried hard to disguise this voice – it is eroded, almost silent within the moment it tries to speak. I can hear the sound behind the voice, of erasure and softness. The information of the voice has been winnowed and tugged at.

It's strange. If you or I wanted to remove a record from the database, we would simply delete the file, I think. But the archive seems not to work in this way. Instead, the voice is made to feel unsure. It has layers of context deleted. The result is something like loneliness. The voice wants to say something, but it no longer has any confidence in itself. So the record shows us a voice without conviction. It has no argument. It has no impact at all. I want to start here. I will have to start again several times.

We will have to keep starting again.

An AV technician speaks

I am speaking. Am I speaking? I don't fully know what this is. The sound in this auditorium is strange. They fucked up the acoustic design, I'm sure of it, way *way* too much dampening on the walls, too much sound absorption generally in this auditorium. It's like a sponge, man.

When I was told there was going to be an expansion of this business park, I got my hopes up. I asked them – will you redo the acoustics in the auditorium then? No, probably not, they said.

Why? I said.

It's just not in the plan. It's a detail, don't ask us about details.

I was in the wrong room, that's what it was. You can't always speak in certain rooms. It's sort of forbidden, if you're me. Jeremiah said I was trying to ask the wrong people. These were senior people, with huge plans.

They weren't sure why I was there. I was there, of course, because they had wanted one of the big screens to work in their boardroom, and that means a technician has to be present. They didn't directly say to me get back to work, but they smiled instead of conversing. They looked away from me, and looked at each other, and I said, 'OK then.' And got on with setting up the screen.

One of them, one of them openly watched me doing this awkward job, stared at me bending over, squatting, struggling with the plugs. Because of them, I started to sweat. It was embarrassing. It's embarrassing to be stared at while you're sweating like that. I don't know why it happens to me, but I am just very sweaty. I think because I stay so hydrated. It's odourless, my sweat, it's not like I am dirty. One of them looked at me in a sort of pitying way, as if to ask if I was OK. If I needed a glass of water – *me!* Look at me, man! I'm a fountain, I don't need water. I didn't say that of course, but with my eyes maybe I did.

I left them to it after the screen was on. Normally I would stay and be on hand, but I just left. I went to a service corridor and looked at my phone. That's what happens when you ask them stuff. When you talk in the wrong context. You feel ridiculous. Like a boy again. This whole situation is infantilising. I'm a child here. If I exist at all.

Anyway, they can't say I didn't warn them about this terrible acoustics situation. I can tell you, they had no idea what they were doing when they set up this carpet on the walls. It's too thick. Nothing leaves it.

You'd go mad if it weren't for the amplification. The sound rig itself is world class. I will concede that. I will concede that now we have worked it out, it's a steady *steady* rack. Too good in fact for a corporate set-up. Way better than they need. These places think they need a stage so they can make their announcements and dance around and cheer like it's an actual gig. They think they're famous now, that's what it is. Businesspeople are the new rock stars, that's what they think. Someone must have come in here to sell them this rig and told them that. Just think how it will feel to stand up there, and project your message in the purest possible sound. They won't even care what you're saying! They won't care that you're reporting profits from sustaining wars all over the world. Controlling water and power. Harvesting the organs of children. They'll think you're a legend!

The harvesting organs thing was a joke, by the way. Sorry (sorry to who? Am I talking? I don't think I am actually talking) – a horrible joke actually. Although, what's a joke when nobody can hear you? What's a joke when it's not even clear you've spoken? No, not even to yourself. Still, an ugly thing to say. Ugh. Even here, Mum (I'm talking to my mum who isn't here), even here, Mum, I'm putting my foot in my mouth, and I have literally no idea if my mouth is even moving or if I'm speaking at all.

It must be a record! That's what we would've said once. Must be a record, Benjamin! Nobody here at all and you've put your foot in it!

No longer do we say these things.

Is my mouth moving? I don't know. I can't move to check these things. I am in the darkness, but if I move I will be seen, and that's not acceptable.

I am way up stage right. That's the back left-hand corner to anyone in the audience. It's not even a real stage. There's no backstage area. There's a lectern, and behind that, a depth of about three metres, several large projection screens, and then the darkness, where we AV technicians hide.

I am hunched and not moving. I came to be in this position because I thought there was a loose wire on the stage, which is potentially catastrophic. People die because of loose wires. So I had to creep from the little stool I had set up right out of the way into this shadow, to fix the wire. But before I could grab it, someone – an assistant I think, like the assistant of the assistant of the CEO – went over to the lectern without telling me or Jeremiah, without any signal at all, full of nervous energy, this assistant cleared their throat and just began talking. Without any cue at all, they just got the whole thing started. Lucky for them the mics were live, otherwise that voice would've died, and everyone would be in a flap. As it was, the show began, and I could not return to my stool.

I've been stuck here since then. This was a long programme of speakers before the main event. First the assistant rambled about some achievement. Then someone from tech gave a talk nobody understood about data lakes. Then the woman from central services who looks after signage and safety, she rambled about the fire escapes being new, about the outer areas of the car park being closed off and prohibited. They have all rambled.

On the stage now is the CEO. There are multiple assistants on the fringes of the light around her, they look at her like she is a god. They do not see me, of course. My back hurts. I had too much coffee this morning. I am worried about my heart. I am worried about my mother. She wears summer clothes that she buys at the market. A bra made of wool. A crochet thing, freezing her skin blue. My sister won't help. What am I supposed to do about this? I have to set it aside – focus on the job, that's what Jeremiah would say. Just focus on the work.

Jeremiah is my colleague, but also my boss really. Jeremiah Sporland. We're together in the dark. He knows much better how everything is meant to be set up. If something breaks, if the sound cuts or the video won't play or the PowerPoint doesn't work, someone will say his name. Multiple people, in fact, will whisper the name of Jeremiah. That's normally what happens anyway. But these people on the stage now, they have no idea who Jeremiah is. They've all come over from the other side of the world. They will stand there in silence, looking relaxed yet burning with anger, until the issue is fixed. We have to fix it in a way that suggests no problem ever existed. The CEO will stop talking. She will stand still, and a few seconds will open up in front of me like a horrible, roaring face. And I will clench up, I will make myself completely passive, nothing will touch me, I won't breathe, I won't move, I won't exist, while Jeremiah fixes the problem.

If this happens, and if Jeremiah cannot fix the microphone, then he will say the words 'Switch mics, Ben.'

This is the cue for me to leap forward and switch the microphone worn by whoever is speaking with the one I am holding around my shoulder. They should not even notice me doing it. I will touch their clothes – the lapel of that blue, blue suit, but not their bodies.

If I do it right, my movements, the action itself, will be so passive, nobody will remember that it happened. The magic connection between speaker and audience, between leader and workforce, will not be broken. It will not exist.

I will not exist.*

I am creeping gently forwards, this is the moment in which the CEO of the company is about to hit her most important notes. I must not distract the CEO at this crucial moment. If the microphone she is wearing is going to break, it is going to break now. If it breaks, her speech will be silent.

---

* **Archivist's note**: The voice almost vanishes here. The volume remains the same, and the sound quality remains the same, but as we have described, the certainty in the voice is weakened here. As though struggling to stay on record, wishing itself away.

I wait. I am holding my breath. It would be now.

Now.

No. It's fine. Or it could still happen, but it's less likely now. If it did happen, there would have been a sound, a kind of chaotic bleep.

I am sweating again, I hope it doesn't glisten. It is completely odourless. It's going into my eyes and blurring everything.

I feel detached. A boy again. I feel like I am looking at something happening in the past. It's the light, and with the salt in my eyes, I feel like I'm crying, which makes me sad I suppose. I cannot see clearly, I no longer see the CEO. I see other things in the light, unreal from here in the dark.

In the corner of the stage is a table, a little set of the room where my father sat when they dismissed him from his job.

The sun was shining on him, only on him, across his neck, across the creases in his dark green blazer, his jeans. I feel like the words have happened already, my father has already received the judgement. This is the moment of silence, in which he must accept the decision of the panel. He will never be allowed to work again in this local authority. They hope he seeks help. He has never told me what happened at this meeting, or why he was forced out of his job. We don't speak much. When I think of him, I think of him in situations like this, on the other side of the divide between the dark, where I sit, and the light, where a blinding scrutiny seems to be taking place, stretching out into an unbearable quiet.

It isn't him, of course, my father is not there on the stage. It's just a CEO about to make an important announcement about expansion. She is a deity at the plinth, with her bottle of still water that cost £10, with hair that is glossy and perfume that is like a cloud.

But I feel like any second I will see him, his little shape on the plastic chair, his hopeless glasses. I'm here, Dad, I want to say. I'm here in the silence. Jeremiah just sniffed. The noise won't have registered on the stage. It's something in the dust, it's been getting up his nose all morning. My back hurts.

The CEO is smiling out and around to the audience. She looks back, though she does not focus on me. I hope she can't hear me talking. I don't think I am talking out loud. I have been doing this for a long time, and Jeremiah hasn't hushed me. And yet I go on.

She is wearing a pale blue suit, the CEO. The way the light hits the suit tells you immediately how much money it must have cost. I will never be able to own a suit of that material, whatever it is. I will never be able to afford it, or even find out where to go to get it. I do not live in the same world as this CEO.

Currently, like every day, I am wearing a black Aertex T-shirt with the logo of the AV technical team on it. It's my skin, it feels like, this T-shirt. Of the five that I own, it is the most new-looking and I wear it on days when I know we have an event in the main auditorium.

It does not catch the light in an expensive way. In fact, it cheapens all light that touches it. If you spill anything, no matter what it is, on this T-shirt, it looks like a semen stain. There has never been semen on this T-shirt, but it looks like I have had nothing to do all day but get semen on myself. I am saying semen a lot. Am I saying it though? What is this? The sound in this room is a mistake. I am right on the edge of the light now. The light has spread because the video is playing, the video about the values of the company where they all work. I suppose these are my values too, since they bought the company I work for. They've bought everything, so I hear, including this whole business park, the trees themselves, the worms in the ground, they have bought it all. Who are these people? That's at least part of the reason for this town hall meeting, I suppose. To reiterate who we all are. There will be a buffet at some point. Like a marriage.

My back is really hurting now.

There are more videos playing. I look round to see the face of Jeremiah, in the distance, just his round head, a look of total concentration. He has just recently got married, last month, and they've bought a house. I went to the wedding, and I think I had a good time, great to be around J and not in the Aertex. Great to be invited and made to feel welcome. There were people there who seemed nice, you know? And I couldn't believe the amount of food there was. I kept thinking about how much money me and Jeremiah make, and wondering how he could be paying for all of this. And since then, on his face, I see that wedding bill. I don't think he paid for it himself, but I think that it is *accounted for*, that whoever paid for it is accounting for it in some future ownership of Jeremiah's soul. I think his wife's parents paid. I think they consider he owes them now, thousands of pounds, tens of thousands of pounds. No wonder he looks so serious. I must have drunk three bottles of champagne, just because it was there. And because I didn't know anybody. At one point, I found myself sat on the edge of the dance floor, just out of the light, in the darkness, and people came whirling past me, someone I might have bumped into earlier would smile and go past. We were in the middle of nowhere, some village that has become a wedding venue, so I couldn't leave. The idea of trudging back to my hotel room felt nauseating, like a waste of the train fare and the hotel bill. But I didn't seem able to connect with anyone really, at that wedding, on that dance floor. They whirled past me, I sat in the darkness just off to the side, if they looked they'd have seen me, but the same way they'd have seen the chairs, or the crumpled napkins, or the pile of coats.

The values of the company are called pillars. The pillars are represented by videos of people making deals, people wearing hard hats.* There's some overspill, which I don't think many people have noticed, but it means the projector is misaligned. Some of the video is cut off from the projection screen, and a face is now somehow projected onto Jeremiah's face. Oh he must hate this.

----

* **Archivist's note:** Recovered and transcribed the following from a screen capture:

• PILLAR 1: UNIVERSALISM – employees chosen to represent universalism walking through a business park. It's not a representation of pre-expansion Capmeadow, so it may be the old headquarters in Texas. (This HQ is also referenced in several hundred archive clippings of expansion meetings – for example, 'When, tell me when did we lose contact with the Texas office? How long has it been since they dialled into these meetings?') The quality of the dentistry also reads as highly American. It also reads as faintly militaristic. A slow, unspoken mist crawls around the ankles of a senior leadership executive.

• PILLAR 2: FLOURISHING – a deal is being made in a boardroom. This time it is definitely in the pre-expansion A building in Capmeadow. The doorway behind the sales manager shaking hands with the client is unusually black. Something flickers there, in the doorway. The client walks with the sales manager through the famous tropical gardens that surround the original buildings of Capmeadow. The dark doorway somehow remains in the background, and seems to get darker.

• PILLAR 3: PROFITABLE – a rapid series of people standing outside palatial office buildings and warehouses, as well as civil projects like bridges, motorways and shipyards. Sometimes the people from the company are wearing hi-vis jackets, sometimes business suits. All of the people pump their fists, all of them, once the camera has them perfectly framed by the building, bridge or ship, they pump their fists, and so do all the people around them.

A successful face. If anyone notices this misalignment, Jeremiah will have to fix it. He will be raging that this misalignment has happened again. I wonder if he will consider it to be my fault. He better not. You better fucking not try and put this on me, Jeremiah! Oh I hate it when he blames me. He never actually says this is your fault, but he just goes all red and blotchy.

He shakes as he bustles around. I will feel like I should be helping, but it's been agreed in advance, if anything happens, I am to just stay out of sight. Stay in the shadows and watch what's happening in the light.

The pain in my back is becoming unbearable. I wonder if anyone else in this room is in pain like this. Just at this moment there must be two thousand people in the audience, and twenty times that on various meeting screens and in other offices around the world. Is anyone, in any of those rooms, I wonder, as close to the brink of agony as I am? I think something has happened to me. When I turned to look at Jeremiah, that must have been when it happened. I have looked away from him now. I don't feel able to turn again and see him. Something has happened. The CEO is speaking again, in the dazzling light. She is saying we are expanding.

We are expanding, Jeremiah! I puff out my cheeks. Can Jeremiah or the CEO hear this? The light is more intense now, I don't recall adding this to the lighting programme, but it is perceptibly brighter now, making the darkness here darker than ever. All I can see is the CEO. All I'm aware of is the CEO. It's just her, and the floating frayed ends of dust from all that carpeting on the walls of the auditorium. The audience in darkness, the suggestion of life, a graveyard at night. I cannot feel my body. I am a shape cut out of sciatica. The light keeps getting brighter, the world darker, my voice is becoming nothing.

I am starting to wonder what would happen if I rose up. If I rose up and started talking, if I announced myself. What would it take, I wonder, for me to exist? Should I step into the light?

I am going to do it. I am going to rise up and be seen. But I don't, of course, I haven't risen up. I don't exist. Nobody can see me. Except.

Except in the audience, I see the face of a man. There is something the matter with his face. There is a terrible worry on him. I can see you! I'm saying with my mind, or with this, whatever voice this is, but of course he can't hear me. Can anyone hear any of this? What is this? What am I doing? But he can.

I think he can hear me. Am I speaking? He is looking straight at me. What has happened to you? I'm asking. The CEO has reached a euphoric level of excitement as she continues to pound on about expansion. The light on her is unbearable. I feel myself rising up.

The sight of this troubled man is immensely disturbing. I don't know how it's possible that I can see him. He should be in darkness, all of them should be in absolute darkness. We must have made a mistake with the lights, Jeremiah. We must have done something wrong, that man's face should be in darkness. His sunken eyes, his terrible hair.

Something unspeakable is happening to that man in the audience. He is talking to me, he is begging me for information. I feel as though the world has changed. I cannot move, I am stuck here forever. I cannot look away from him. I feel sure that something very bad is happening. Why else would I be frozen like this? Why else would I have seen my father or evidence of my mother's illness, seen it when I could not help them? How can I help anyone? I get no help, am I dying? Is he here to take me away?

If I could just stand up, I would be alive again.*

Tom Crowley continues to arrive at work

'Feeling OK?' I said. We had arrived and had gone through the barriers, and were now outside the train station. There were elements of the walk out of the station, the last few stops on the train, that were a blur.

'I said are you feeling OK, Hen?'

'Yes.'

'Sorry for shouting.'

'It's OK.'

'I'm trying my best.'

'I know.'

It was a ten-minute wait at the taxi rank for the shuttle bus. As Hen skipped along the pavement, on the kerb, off the kerb, on the kerb again, I texted Eliane.

Lost my shit on the train, I wrote. Feel dreadful, but she was just relentlessly pushing. I don't think it was that bad. #fuckingkids.

I didn't have any signal, and the text failed to send. I never figured out what happened to that text. Eliane said that she never received it.

'Is it far from here?' Hen asked. I put my phone away. The

sun was behind her, I couldn't see her face clearly, everything became blotchy.

'Not far, no,' I said.

'Why don't we walk?'

'You never want to walk anywhere.'

'I always want to walk! It's you who always say no.'

'I'm shocked!' I said. 'I'm shocked that you want to walk, but we can't today.'

She kept skipping in and out of the sunlight, her shape then blotches crawling across my vision. I looked away from her, back down at the phone, trying to find out where we were meant to be going.

'So shall we walk, Daddy?'

'We could, but we'd be late. I want us to have time to see my desk before you go off and learn to code!'

The email had definitely said she would learn to code, I was sure of it. But the email wasn't there – I continued scrolling, but I couldn't find anything, the blotches from the sun swam over everything. I put my phone away.

I got it out again. I searched again. Nothing. I opened an email to send to someone but I didn't know who to write to. Hen was chasing pigeons. Other workers were gathering around the pickup space where the next shuttle bus would arrive. I could see Hen between the smart autumn coats of a group of obvious graduate programme alumni. They spoke the language of the place in a way that felt beyond me. For example, it is impossible that they didn't know who I could talk to about Bring Your Daughter to Work Day, but actually approaching them was out of the question. Some shimmering barrier existed between them and me, of fine navy wool and pale gabardine, of perfume and knowledge of the managerial class that runs the company. They used first names for senior managers, seemed to know the movements of decision-makers.

'I got eleven emails from her this morning,' one of them said. 'I can't believe she's going to go on stage and talk after last night.'

'Oh my god, I left early – what happened? What?'

'You left before she started ordering tequila?'

'I don't remember tequila. I had Jack calling me relentlessly, remember?'

'Jesus. It was so messy.'

'Jack never turned up.'

They occasionally looked round at me, breaking out, one face at a time, from the huddle to regard the world around them, to make sure they were not about to trip over my legs, or spill their coffees. Each time one of them peeped out like this, their huddle got tighter, the speech more whispered and more urgent. Mist from the combined breath of the circle rose up and rushed away. A shuttle bus arrived, they all got in, there was no option for me to check if I could join them. They didn't want me in there, and I didn't want to get in. Through the windows of the bus, their faces rationalised into the professional expressions they would wear all day. They did not look as though they were breathing.

The next shuttle bus was along five minutes later. Just in case you don't remember the old shuttle buses, they were basically school minibuses but they ran on electricity – all day they went from the station to the Capmeadow campus. Sometimes they'd go on a longer route and take in Titan Court, but this won't mean anything to you at all now. Titan Court was released long ago. I know this because I was asked to help with the messaging of the decommissioned areas and with the requests that conversations about Titan Court should be removed from ongoing chats and archived using the attached instructions.

Hen loved the shuttlebus. It made the sound of string instruments in the cold. After a few minutes, we reached the lower flats where the mist came in. Buildings and complexes stood out as correlations of red lights that tracked the shapes of their cranes. Construction work in that zone was constant. White lights blinked at mountain height in the distance to demonstrate the campus parks of Woodford, Jupiter Centre, Killmarsh and so on. Hotels blinked green. Closer to, you'd see other shuttles, light traffic – all branded up or belonging to building companies. The roads were always private. You could walk there, but it was a risk in the fog. You could cycle, but not many people bothered.

'It's foggy!' Hen said as the electric shuttlebus violined us towards Capmeadow.

'Yes, it's a thick one today,' I said, joining her to watch the greyness fold through the various roundabouts, checkpoints and private roads of the other business parks that pocked the landscape out near Capmeadow.

'There's people in it,' Hen said.

I couldn't see anyone, but I didn't have time to ask what she meant before the driver piped up.

'Always mist in the morning,' he said over his shoulder. 'Good for the salvias.'

'What's a salvia?' Hen asked.

'A flower,' I said. 'You'll see them when we get there.'

I watched Hen trying to penetrate the grey block on the other side of the window. 'I want to see a salvia,' she said. 'What colour are they?' But the sun was the only thing cutting through.

I often just make a noise when my kids ask me a question. She asked me what colour this plant was. I heard her ask. She asked me the colour of a flower – the sort of thing you imagine will be part of the idyllic life, describing the colours of a flower to your inquisitive, inexhaustible, deeply wondrous child, but in the event I just needed to have some peace, so I didn't answer. We looked out of the window.

'I hope they're OK,' Hen said after a few minutes.

'The flowers?' I asked.

'They love it,' the driver said.

'No, not the flowers, the people.'

'What people?' I said. 'There are no people.'

'I can see them in the mist. Grownups and children. They are holding hands'

I looked harder out of the window, which only served to remind me I was probably going blind. I could feel the muscles in my eyes failing as I tried to make out shapes of people in the milk outside the shuttle bus.

'Maybe they are here for the bring your daughter to work day too!' she said.

'Nobody out here,' the driver said. It was weird to me how sure he sounded. 'Everyone knows it's not safe to be out here.'

'There's nothing there, Hen,' I said.

After the argument on the train, she was already sitting further from me than usual. She didn't respond, just kept looking out.

I looked for children with adults, but there was nothing. Air the colour of salt. The powerless sun appearing as a coin.

The driver enjoyed having Hen in the bus. He talked to her more about the plants in the mist. 'Get your old dad to show you around. Make sure now.'

'Which entrance are we going to?' I asked, noticing the bus had taken a slightly different route. I panicked that we might be on our way to the C building entrance, which was bloody miles away.

'Main entrance, Building B.'

'Oh the main entrance, Hen. That's special. We normally come in round the back.'

Hen was beaming. 'Are these the big doors?' she asked the driver.

'That's right, just like I said.'

I hadn't heard them discussing the main entrance or the big doors. But here we were. We entered Building B through the big revolving doors – normally the big doors are for visitors and clients. They're the kind of thing that are irritating and slow as an adult, but to a kid, you can see they resemble a roundabout at the park.

I looked at Hen's hand on the door as she pushed round, the size of it. She will always seem so small to me, her hands especially. New parents talk about their babies' hands all the time, but maybe we don't talk about the continuation of this. My son has feet like a yeti, but if I saw them sticking out the end of his bed in the morning, I'd want to touch them, and remember when they were smaller than a hotel soap bar. Little pink pads with nodes attached. His hands, I'd hold my son's hands in my hands as often as I could.

Whenever I was close enough, I'd touch the back of his head, his hair like feathers. His smell like sour milk. I've never stopped wanting to hold all of these things close to me.

I went twice round the revolving doors just to make Hen laugh, just to keep seeing her hand on the door. We annoyed a man I didn't recognise, but who I also felt sure was no threat to me. I imagined being in an HR meeting with the man and not even having to say anything while he complained about me pushing the revolving door round a bit faster than usual to amuse my daughter, I saw the HR specialists concealing grins. All of us in on the joke and then getting back to work without a mark against my name.

There were no other children in the lobby. I registered this fact, and then immediately let it drop away from me. While I went to the reception desk, Hen made herself known. She methodically sat on each of the three deep waiting-area sofas, one at a time, crashing gently onto every dim burgundy cushion. She spread her arms out, sighing as she landed, and I could hear her gently say 'Smoosh.'

'Come on, Hen,' I said. 'I need you over here.'

'Just a second,' she sang, striding away in the opposite direction, down the long stretch of marble, smiling at the security guards, dodging traffic at the turnstiles.

'It's Bring Your Daughter to Work Day,' I said to the receptionists at large, but nobody responded. There were three of them all in a row, and each one had on a headset. They were focusing on the screens in front of them. It was impossible to tell whether they were on a call or just responding to email, or simply frozen like that, looking at nothing.

'I'm pretty sure it is,' I said again, choosing a single receptionist to address this time.

The receptionist I chose looked older than the others, more tired and therefore, to me anyway, more understanding. According to his name badge, he was called Steve. I should have known this. Steve had let me in multiple times when I'd forgotten my lanyard. Steve. I resolved to keep his name in my head this time. Steve.

'Sorry, how can I help, sir?' said Steve. 'Don't tell me you forgot your ID again?'

'Aha! No, not this time,' I said. I dangled out my ID card. 'No, I need to sign that one in, over there.'

Steve looked off into the marble concourse. He seemed confused. Hen was not there.

'Oh she's probably lying on the ground. Hen! Where are you? Sorry, Steve. What I'm trying to say is that I think it's Bring Your Daughter to Work Day? That's why I've got my daughter with me. She's over there somewhere.'

'Hmm,' said Steve, and hunched his shoulders, glaring at his screen as if peering at something written in tiny print.

I glared across the lobby at Hen, who was back, and now lying on an armchair with her toes on a low coffee table.

'Feet off the table, please!' I said.

The table looked like it cost more than my annual salary, but I didn't raise my voice when she refused to remove her feet. The company had told us we could bring in our daughters – we couldn't be expected to make them stop being children suddenly. They surely must have expected a certain amount of scuffing of coffee tables.

Contrary to everything I knew about small children, I told myself that she was too small to do any real damage.

'Hmm,' said Steve again, still peering at his screen. 'Hmm.' The sound seemed like it was going on for a long time.

'All OK?' I said.

'Oh yes, all good,' said Steve.

'Phew! I thought you were going to tell me you can't find any record of Bring Your Daughter to Work Day!'

'Well, so far, I can't. I'm still just looking. But it *must* be in here somewhere if you say it is. And you have an email, you said, so it must be . . . Can I see that email actually?'

'Oh. I'm afraid I seem to have deleted the email. I'll look again.'

'If you could, sir. At present, I don't have anything in the system about any daughters to work day. Is this a firmwide scheme?'

I could feel my skin going cold.

'I don't know,' I said. 'I work in the engineering division. So might just be a technology thing?'

Steve made a noise in his throat like he was swallowing half a pint of milk. He peered at the screen, hidden from my view. He tapped the desk and peered again. I started to wonder if one of the other, younger, more intimidating receptionists would've been more helpful or less flummoxed by the technology.

'Nothing there?' I asked.

Steve came to a stop and looked up from his screen, defeated at last. 'No, it's not in my system,' he said. 'But that doesn't mean much. We're always the last to know!'

I rolled my eyes and tutted. 'This place! I don't know sometimes how we even do business with all this chaos.'

'Exactly.'

'What should I do then, Steve? Do you need to call anyone or? I mean, can I still take her in?'

'Call someone? No, there's no need to call anyone — we don't even know who to call, do we? Who would you call? No, no. We'll just sort her a pass and then you can go in.'

Steve slowly raised the index finger of his left hand and touched the corner of his mouth, at the same time opening his face into a sudden blazing smile.

All the lights went out. Steve vanished.

For a second I couldn't see anything at all. I wasn't even sure of the ground beneath my feet. My whole body was numb, I felt the blood in my face swell like a bruise. I could hear a roaring oceanic pressure, it was too much, I thought I would literally split open. And then, as this sensation felt like it couldn't get any worse, there came an easing. The swelling and the numbness went away. But the darkness remained.

I called out to Hen, 'Hey, are you OK?'

There was no answer, but it was typical of her to go silent in the dark like this. Her normal reaction to something frightening is to freeze completely. 'Don't worry chicken! It's just a power cut, it will be OK in a minute. I'm here, I'm here.' I kept saying it, and she made no sound back, so I kept saying it, I'm here. I am right here.

'What's happening, Steve?' I said. There was no answer from him. I could not see where his shape had been.

From somewhere, a red light came on. The reception area was visible but transformed by the light. The furniture was now a series of black oblongs, people became pillars, became people and back again, I wasn't sure of anything I could see. Nothing moved. The banking mist rolled against the glass panels and the doors, red light moved, like milk in black coffee.

'I'm here, Hen,' I said, my voice catching for some reason. 'I'm right here, Hen.'

When the lights came back, she was next to me again. She was looking up at Steve. Nobody in the lobby seemed at all phased, but it did not feel right to speak yet. There was a kind of professional glaze over everything, and it felt like it would be inappropriate to mention it.

'That was weird,' I said.

Steve smiled.

'These power cuts have been on and off for a while,' he said.

Somehow knowing that here was an adult who was going to give her something, Hen tapped the reception desk with her boot. Steve looked down at her for the first time.

'Welcome to Capmeadow!' he said, spreading his arms out wide, glowing with that cinematic smile that had opened up his face before the lights went out. 'Do you mind if I take your picture, madam?'

'Sure!' said Hen.

'I thought I'd lost you,' I said. She didn't hear me. I barely felt like I was there. My feet felt like they were gently rising and then returning to the ground. I had been so tired. I remembered my kitchen, the emptiness of it. What happened next required nothing from me, and I felt unable to take part in it.

Steve stood up, plucking the webcam that had been resting on the top of his monitor.

'Smile please!' he said to Hen.

She beamed up at him. He made the clicking sound of a photograph being taken with his mouth because the webcam camera itself didn't make a noise. 'Beautiful,' Steve said.

I confirmed Hen's name and our address, which Steve processed instantly, and then all his attention was back on Hen.

'How old are you, love?'

'Eight.'

'Eight years old! And what do we call you?'

'Hen.'

'Like a chicken? Or like Henrietta?'

'It's not Henrietta at all!'

She gave this little routine to anyone who asked her name. We all call her Hen, but it's got nothing to do with her real name, she's not Henrietta, which most people assume. There isn't even a good story around it.

When she was a baby, her head would sometimes look strangely thin, especially when she was having her hair washed. It wasn't only that it was a small head, it was also such a thin one, and we called her Hen because she had the head of a chicken when she was there in the bath, with her dark eyeballs glancing around, smiling back because we were so delighted with her mindless expression and her narrow little head. We said it so much that it became her name, became what her friends at school call her, her teachers.

While she explained her hen-headedness to Steve, I was flipping through emails and my calendar on my phone. I was so sure I had this date right. I'd told everyone. Booked Hen out of school. Negotiated a credit for her afterschool care. I felt sure I had done everything properly. I could hear Steve saying the fog lifts and rolls away and leaves everything clean. He was saying that the flowers love it, naming flowers I didn't know. Hen, too, was describing hellebores and other varieties of flower I did not realise she knew about. The tropical gardens, Steve was saying, were the reason he and his wife moved here. A good job – that was of course the first reason they had moved here. A good pension, affordable housing in a nice area, but the topper – the icing on the cake – a job looking out over those beautiful gardens. And she would come, Joan would come, he was saying, and on his lunch break they would just sit and admire the natural miracle of the mist. The mist is a miracle, he was saying. I could hear him. And I could hear my daughter too, involved, talking like an adult, but I could not look away from the screen of my phone. Nothing I was looking at made any sense.

I couldn't find any trace of Bring Your Daughter to Work Day. I was getting a headache. The shapes were still returning to normal after the blackout. The room felt bigger, the walls stained somehow, as though years ago a great flood had come in and rolled away, leaving marks of itself, adhering age to the fittings and the walls. Someone somewhere was coughing. Outside, the sun was too bright. The car park seemed to have been eaten by the ranging shadows of the tropical gardens that lay beyond. My head throbbed.

'Oh god,' I said. 'Fucksake.' Nobody listened to me.

She was there with me, but I thought of Hen's face, her way of pressing all her feelings into her cheeks, and how sadness never stays inside of her for long. I could see that overspilling of her confusion and then acceptance and foaming disappoint-ment. She was standing there, I could almost touch her, but I was picturing her, almost in tears at the thought of letting her down again.

This was the moment I realised that I hadn't necessarily told Eliane that I was taking Hen out of school at all. I felt quite hot suddenly. I checked the next year in my calendar, in case I had added it incorrectly. This has happened before. I have booked restaurants a year in advance. It wasn't in the calendar. It did not appear in any of our messages on various platforms. Nobody had been at home when we got up. Why had I thought this was happening today? When had I been told about it?

'Daddy!' Hen was poking at my hip with something sharp. I looked away from my phone, having given up on finding any record of it ever being Bring Your Daughter to Work Day.

'Look!' She was holding up her newly printed ID card.

'Ah brilliant!' I said. 'A picture of a monkey!'

'It's me!'

'What? Let me see that!' She's beaming in the photo, her teeth like pale stones in her tiny head. In the background are the looming marble pillars of the lobby. In the distance, the blacked-out lift vestibule. The whole thing looks drowned. I held it in my hands, I touched the corners of it, felt the flex. She had it around her neck like a medal.

Steve on reception put his soft hand on my shoulder.

'Oh man, I've got a bad feeling, Steve,' I said.

'Don't worry. She's booked in, you've followed all the correct protocol. I don't know about any Bring Your Daughter to Work Day, but she can now safely access your floor and the canteen areas on seven, twenty-one, thirty-three and forty-five.'

'I doubt we'll be going to forty-five,' I said.

'Ha, oh yeah, fair enough!'

If Hen wondered why Steve and I were laughing at the idea of going to the forty-fifth floor, she didn't show it, she just laughed along with us.

There had been a notorious event or a leak up there. It wasn't ever made clear what exactly happened. Nobody had visited the forty-fifth floor for about three months. Emails reminding us it was out of bounds kept coming – which was strange. It wasn't as if we could get through the locked doors, the lift that wouldn't stop there, or the fire stairwell that was boarded up and taped over. And there was a guide I had been asked to write, something outside my normal training design remit, on what to do if someone you know or someone you suspect has been using the forty-fifth floor. It was a weird thing to have to write. Cath Corbett, who commissioned the work, just said it was an overreaction to some people who had prised back the boarded-up doors and had been using the forty-fifth floor as an informal place to meet after work.

But who was meeting on the forty-fifth floor after work informally? I asked. Cath Corbett had shrugged. It had been where the pool and table tennis facilities were housed, but they were quite shit. It didn't seem serious that people were breaking in there to hang out. When I pressed Cath Corbett about this, she sighed at me and in a testy voice reminded me that the fridges had been stocked with lager and prosecco.

She seemed not to want to press the issue. Maybe people were breaking in to try and find out why it was out of bounds? I asked this and she said it wasn't that. It was informal gathering and just write the training as a priority please.

I let it go – what did I care? I was asked to write a lot of strange instructions back then. 'Give it to Tom' seemed to be the policy. He literally can't say no. He is so disorganised, he won't know how much or how little work he has on anyway.

*

I let Hen press the button for the lift up to third, where I had my desk at that time. In the lift her hand slipped back into mine. A moment to recharge, which was her way of saying it. She needed to recharge when she was nervous. A hug or holding hands did the trick. It was cute, but of course she'd do it when it was dinner time, and this lost its charm when one mouthful of food took thirty minutes and endless baby-voiced hugs.

I shook at that guilt again. I tried to leave it in the lift, though of course it followed me like a mugger wherever I went, the guilt and the anger and the piss-poor resilience.

It was funny watching her interact with the people in the office. I became a tour guide, and my colleagues monuments of varying intrigue. 'Here is Matilda, we work together. Say hello.'

'Hello!'

'Hello!'

The surprised faces of my colleagues became more and more alarming – especially those who I felt sure would be with their own daughters.

'Let's find Alex,' I said to Hen.

'Who's Alex?'

'Alex Wood – I told you; he has a daughter your age. She might be here.'

'OK.'

I was lying about the age of Alex Wood's daughter. She was six, I felt sure. Or maybe seven. But old enough to be here, and he would be certain to bring her, I felt sure. If there's an extra-work activity, Alex Wood is there, up to his elbows in banter, dressed as a Christmas elf, ready to win the charity egg-and-spoon race.

My natural instinct is to avoid talking to Wood. I always feel like I'm interrupting him. He has this way of turning his head away from his screen really slowly, like he's literally dragging himself away from his emails to look at me. And then it's all an inconvenience to him, my pleasantries.

'Hi Alex! Hen, this is Alex Wood,' I said.

'Hi,' said Wood, stooping over to greet her. He seemed surprised to see a kid in the office. 'Are you off school then?' he said in a slightly grating goofish voice. 'Teacher training day?'

'It's uh, Bring Your Daughter to Work Day, in fact,' I said.

Alex raised an eyebrow. 'What? Fudge! I didn't know about it. Ah man, I could've brought Lucy in.'

'This is becoming a theme,' I said. 'Nobody else seems to know about it.'

'Oh right.' Alex immediately shifted from worried he was missing out, to calmly knowing that I had fucked up again.

'Yeah,' I said. 'I seem to be the only one.'

I looked around at people going about their business, staring at screens, looking at their phones or their hands or the space above their screens or just some natural mental zone they stared at when in the office. Conspicuously not jockeying kids around or doing performed gentle parenting.

'I'm beginning to wonder if I imagined it,' I said.

'Yeesh,' Wood said.

'What am I going to do?'

'Oh mate! I don't know what to say.'

'She's expecting this whole day of stuff. I told her there was a coding academy and some kind of presentation. Like, does any of this sound like it's real? It's almost definitely not real . . .'

Hen was wandering the line of mostly unoccupied desks. Alex Wood looked extremely keen to not be talking to me any more.

'No no mate, don't stress. You probably got it right. I really wouldn't pay any attention to me at the moment, I've got no idea what's going on here. I'm not your guy!'

Hen was playing with a pair of headphones at one of the empty desks. I had spent a lot of time over the previous days drilling her on what she could and couldn't do at the office. We made lists, which she decorated, I saw her decorate them, drawing and redrawing animals, rabbits, hearts and phones, my circular face, beard, glasses, a smile I felt like she can't have seen often enough. The list was agreed, it was ours, and we both had listed the rules.

Can:
- Be polite
- Eat one chocolate croissant
- Ask questions if someone has said they have time to talk
- Listen to grownups
- Eat whatever you like from the canteen
- Sit next to the window in the high-up meeting room

Can't:
- Spin on the chairs
- Go where I can't see you
- Mess around with other people's equipment
- Play with my phone without permission

'No – I've fucked up, Alex' I said. 'Nobody else has their kids with them.'

'I don't even know who has kids here to be honest, I'm sure it's fine.'

'No, no I've fucked it. There'd be like, banners or something, some colouring stuff. I don't know. The ops team in special T-shirts . . .'

Alex shrugged. 'Sorry mate,' he said.

49

We stood there for a moment before Wood slowly turned back to his screen.

'Maybe I'll just take her back home,' I said, leaning round to get into Wood's peripheral vision. 'I can get her to school by lunch and . . .'

'I wouldn't leave now,' Wood said.

'Why?'

'You haven't seen the email? There's a town hall – all hands – in person – downstairs.'

'Fuck, really?'

Wood nodded. Last time there had been one of these town halls was in February. We called it the Valentine's massacre because huge swathes of the technology team and design ops were sacked.

'Is it in the auditorium?'

'Uh-huh.'

'I can't take her down there.'

'Nope.'

'Fuck.'

'Hi there! Sorry I'm late. Crazy on this floor today!'

Wood had joined a call while I was standing there behind him. I looked at his screen. There were a few people I recognised. I fought back the urge to wave. I could see myself over Wood's shoulder on the screen: a transgressor with grease spots on his pale yellow sweater. Instinctively I reached up a hand to try and do something about my hair and then, seeing him grimace on screen, I stepped out of the line of Wood's camera.

Of course, when I looked round for her, Hen had vanished.

I walked casually down the aisle between the wide rows of desks. Hen-level disturbances would be easy to spot. I knew she wouldn't leave the floor, but still I felt the slow panic coming on. A supermarket form of dread – you expect to find the lost child in the next aisle, but the next aisle is empty, so you push on to the next, where, surely, they will be, holding a large bag of crisps no doubt or a bar of chocolate, but the crisps and the chocolate aisles are empty, and the final shelves are coming up, and there are not enough aisles left to give you hope.

You begin to imagine someone taking her by the hand, a face leaning in with a smile and biting at her ear with a threat, and blood rushes loudly in your ears, a rage you recognise but cannot name, your arteries open up, something washes around the edge of your vision, and then there she is by the grapes. By the grapes all along!

Except, she was not there, in the office, I couldn't see her at all.

I did another full sweep without seeing her. And then back again. I was laughing and shaking my head. I went to the ladies' bathroom and called in through the door.

'Sorry,' I said to the analyst who emerged looking confused. 'Did you see my daughter in there? She's about this tall. Wearing dungarees.'

'No, sorry, it was empty,' said the analyst. She clearly wanted to get back to her desk.

'Ah, thanks,' I said. 'Sorry.'

'Sorry,' said the analyst. She still didn't move away. I had this horrible peripheral sense that I was trapping her there.

'It's meant to be Bring Your Daughter to Work Day,' I said.

'Oh, I see.'

'Have you heard about it?'

'No, sorry.'

Back on the office floor, someone was calling my name. I couldn't see where the voice was coming from, but I knew that it was Cath Corbett – and I knew for sure that Hen would have found her and recognised her from our many video calls I've had with Cath Corbett from the kitchen table at home.

I felt an unexpected relief wash through me as I turned towards Cath's voice. I smiled and began to apologise for any inconvenience my child may have caused. But Cath Corbett was alone at her desk. She was looking concerned. Some of my work was open on her computer screen.

'Have you seen her?' I started to say, but Cath Corbett ignored me. Or didn't really hear. She talked over me, clearly annoyed.

'Er, sorry, Tom, are you able to take a look at this?' Cath asked.

'Oh – uh, I thought—'

'Are you all right?'

'Ugh, yes, sorry, sorry Cath. How are you?'

'Fine thanks. Can you look at this document you shared on Friday? We went over it this morning with the DDP team, and they had a *lot* of questions.'

'Oh, right, I did explain it was just a first draft. What did they say?'

'Don't have time to get into it now, I sent you the notes. If you can look at them before the afternoon, then get back to DDP. It's just – oh look, it's too complicated to explain. I'll show you.'

Just to explain, Cath Corbett was not technically my boss, but the way it worked, she was reporting back to my boss on the material I was producing for her team. She was like a client. I was glancing over my shoulder while she talked, seeing flickers of where Hen might have gone.

At last, I saw Hen. She was way down the other end of the office space, moving from desk to desk, her chin high. She had her most determined face, looking simultaneously ready to take on the world and to burst into tears. As always, she moved as a different shape to the people around her, brighter and more fluid than any other form in the office. At least, this is how I saw her. It's fairly difficult to know how the rest of the world would have seen it, but to me, she was like a blaze in the presence of others.

I felt my shoulders relax and then immediately tense up as a new stupid anger flared – where had she been? At this moment, I felt like I was doing some amazing parenting just because I wasn't rushing down the length of the office towards her, ready with harshly whispered admonitions. A voice inside my head told me to let her make her own way. It is boring in an office. Just relax and let her come back to you, the voice said. It was a long way, maybe a thirty-to-forty-second walk.

I allowed myself not to track her. I turned away from Hen and made myself focus on what Cath Corbett was saying. On her three screens were open slides representing the work I had been doing for the last three weeks. It amounted to very little actual work, and I had been going agonisingly slowly, with little engagement with the brief. It was, frankly, bad work. I had been detached for months. Cath was talking while I tried to focus on the words she was showing me. I was waiting for the clasp of my daughter's hand, and wondering why it still had not come.

'Here, you see? These descriptions you've given us for the artwork. Is this right?'

Cath was pointing at words. I could not read the words. My hand remained daughterless.

'How do you mean? Sorry, which project is this, Cath?'

Cath looked at me with naked exasperation. She all but rolled her eyes. She took a breath and started again.

'This is supposed to be the images brief for the fire safety uplift work. These are your descriptions for the illustrators to work with.'

'Oh yeah, right.' Hen was still not there. I looked at my terrible work, and could not see the words.

'Right, so. It says here the managers are cowering in the lobby?'

I mouthed cowering in the lobby and tried to look at what she was talking about.

'Tom. Why are they cowering in the lobby?'

'Yeah sorry,' I said. 'So, if I remember rightly, they've gone to the wrong assembly point. Right? We agreed there should be a team who make the wrong decision.'

'Well, yeah we did say that, but I don't think managers cowering in the lobby is what I asked for.'

'Well, it's just a description for the art team to find the right image.'

'We already have plenty of stock images of grouped teams.'

'I just put what I think you would have if a group of managers were trapped in the wrong place during an emergency incident. I can change it.'

'Good. Change it. Can you also change this one?'

'Yeah OK, sure. Apologies, I think I can review all these descriptions.'

'No. No, we can't waste any more time. Just get these two changed and let's move on.'

'Fine, Cath, leave this with me – I'll get it sorted.'

I headed away from Cath Corbett's desk in a hurry. At the far end of the room, standing by the doors, looking small and sad, was Hen.

I waved and mouthed, 'Stay where you are,' as I rushed towards her. I could feel the faces of other workers turning towards me, like melons cut in half, blank yet judgemental. I tried to sound calm when I finally held her hand again.

'I'm going to get us a meeting room, OK?' I said.

'Sure.'

'I'll get us a meeting room and you can sit in the meeting room and do some drawing, OK? I'm very sorry this is not what you were expecting.'

'It's OK, Daddy,' she said. She was holding Picolo. Both she and the stuffed animal were enough to make me want to cry.

I led her to my desk, letting her wave at people as we went. Letting Cath Corbett see what I was dealing with today. Cath Corbett didn't seem to notice Hen. She just turned away from me, unflinchingly fucked off.

I finally opened my laptop and did what I should've done when I arrived. I messaged Jo, the office manager.

'I'm getting us a room with a big window,' I said to Hen as I begged Jo to explain what was happening, and watched the dots of Jo's replies coming in.

- Jo – please tell me it's Bring Your Daughter to Work Day.
- What? What's Bring Your Daughter to Work Day?
- Don't joke around, Jo! Tell me I haven't imagined it.
  I am sure it's today.
- Sorry, Tom. I don't know who told you that.
  Did you dream it?
- It's not Bring Your Daughter to Work Day, then?
- No!
- Oh God. Then, sorry, but I need to book a room. Sorry, I f***ed up! I've got my kid with me.
- Ha oh Jesus, Tom. This is classic.
- I know I know I'm sorry I'll get you a coffee to say thank you.
- Nevermind – go to meeting room 3 in the corner.

I led Hen to the corner of the office floor, to the small meeting room that nobody ever books because you can only fit two people in there and it smells weird after about five minutes of the door being shut.

'It's not really Bring Your Daughter to Work Day,' I said when we arrived in the corner office. 'I'm so sorry.'

'I know,' Hen said.

'At least that means you're the only one.'

'Yeah.'

'So it's special. Right?'

She said nothing. Picolo, now being held up to glare at me, also said nothing.

'OK, Hen, try not to be sad. I'll move all my work so I can hang with you, but first there is a meeting downstairs I have to go to. Is that all right?'

'Sure!'

'I'll be really quick.'

'Don't worry!'

I gave her some paper and let her use my laptop to play solitaire.

I sat with her for a while, replying to emails on my phone, sending apologies, cancelling meetings I had scheduled in for the afternoon – making it clear in my apologies that possibly the town hall would mean all meetings were cancelled anyway – something to lessen the blow. I didn't bother looking for any more evidence of Bring Your Daughter to Work Day.

'I have to go to the bathroom,' I said to Hen. 'I haven't been since we got here. Do you need to go?'

'I've been to the toilet like five times already, Daddy.'

'Really?'

'Yeah!'

'OK, well I have to go. I'll be really quick.'

'OK.'

'You have to stay here.'

'OK.'

Of course, when I got back from the toilet, she was gone. And properly gone this time. I did not find her again.

Steve from reception speaks

Of course I looked for that girl. A lot of us were looking for her, except those who were at the expansion town hall in the auditorium. Back then, it was endless meetings about the expansion project, you got to the point where you couldn't tell one day from the next, but of course I remember that girl. Of course we looked for her.

But I was the only one who had done any training. The only one who even knew how to conduct a proper search. Before I got involved, it was just corporate people, no offence, but, you know, people with desk jobs who don't know how to organise a proper search party. They don't know the method. So yeah – a lot of people were looking, but I was maybe the first person to really *search* for this girl.

It was also thanks to me that we were able to show pretty much for certain that she wasn't anywhere in the building. I was the only one, which is mad because I shouldn't even have been working, the way I was at that time. I should've been signed off, that's the truth.

Things were bad. I'd been living, like, on the surface of my life.

Listen. Every Friday, I used to get eggs from a farm not far from where I was living. It was a family farm. I only met the family a couple of times. I'd only lived in the village for a couple of years, which made me a complete outsider as far as they were concerned. I was known and had friends, but there are so many layers to the people who live in those isolated places. You can never hope to know them after just a couple of years. Also, I was a solitary person. I moved there to be a solitary person. A picture of Joan, and not much else. I was good for the eggs, though. I paid more than asking. I always returned my boxes undamaged to be used again. After a while, they'd leave me my own personalised box. Stephen, it said. Not how it's spelt, but I don't mind. I'd put as much as I could into the honesty box. Much more than you'd pay in the supermarket, but I never had many outgoings, especially then. The eggs were absolutely delicious. Yolks like a sun inside and the white had this silver gilt. I was mesmerised just mixing them, watching them settle and blend. Powerful eggs.

One day a sickness came to the farm. Terrible. Devastating for the livestock. The lovely hens all had to be kept inside, but they still produced eggs. I continued to pay the old price for them, even though many people stayed away, and the quality was bound to diminish.

The eggs were still delicious, but the shells were thin. Your thumb'd go through if you didn't handle them carefully. The first time I crushed one of those eggs in my hand, without even striking the mixing bowl, I realised that I was just the same. A sick egg. The surface I was living on was set to break at any moment. That's the emotional state I was in when we heard about the missing girl.

The man, Tom, he was going through something very strange. In my opinion he was lucky not to get sacked.

There was a period in the aftermath of all this where we had to physically stop him coming back into the office. Despite all the evidence, he said she was still here. He was convinced he would find her somewhere in the grounds or, one time, it was the heating ducts.

Big problem for me. It would only become an HR issue if he touched the doors, you know, the biometrics would show up. So I would be out there in the garden to prevent him coming in. A few times I had to rescue him from the planters late at night.

I didn't really know him before all of this happened. He asked for me, which I don't understand, on the day she went missing. Or he said she went missing. I don't understand that either. I don't understand a lot of things to be honest.

Last night, for example, I went to bed and when I woke up this morning, new grass. New grass all along the avenue outside the hotel room where I've been staying. Did they come in the night? Only I think we ought to know the species of grass, if you're going to be laying turf in the middle of the night, it's only fair to let us know what kind of grass it is.

[A voice: Would you like me to find out what kind of grass it is?]

It's a bit late now! All I mean is, some of us might have allergies. You should be thinking about that in advance. Or we might have had ideas. We might have wanted to make a suggestion about the use of the grass. As I mentioned, before I moved into the hotel, I was a rural tenant. I might have knowledge that'd be of use next time, with specific reference to the uses of the grass. Like ornamental lawn versus a meadow mix, something that can grow a bit more wild, some texture. Just a thought, of course. I'm still capable of them from time to time. Anyway, enough of this. I bore myself shitless. The point I was making is that this man, this Tom, he was prone to strange behaviour and trespassing.

You know, he was obviously having some kind of delusional event. He was convinced that I had met his daughter, but as you know, there's no record of her in the system.

'Tom, mate,' I said. 'This has to end. You're risking your job here.'

He wasn't bothered. 'What's a job? She's gone.'

'She's at home,' I said. 'Your little girl's been at home all along.'

He just looked at me. A sort of smile on his face like I was the one who was insane. I had my own problems, but I was nowhere near as bad as him. He was a broken man. I would have left him well alone, but he kept asking for me. He seemed to think I was something to do with it all.

On the day she went missing, he called for me. Get Steve, he had apparently said. I was pissed off, pardon me for swearing, but it was the end of my shift on the front desk. I wanted to go home and lock in some Lemsip.

I'd had this migraine all morning, huge groups of delegates in, the CEO and her mob, sorry, executive support team, as you say, all of it happening and I was just getting out the other side of it all.

I didn't remember any kid coming in, but if he said I had met her, then I couldn't really argue. I took a breath and went to find him, to ask what I could do. That was when I realised there was no organisation at all – just office workers wandering around a building, half of them went to get coffee during the search, did you know that? Half! And Tom, the man himself, the bereft man, he went into the town hall with the bloody CEO.

Anyway, instead of wasting time mooching along the corridors, I got into the CCTV room and we started spooling through everything.

We checked all the security footage of the foyer area. There was nothing on there. No sign of Tom coming in with any girl. Although, there was actually no sign of Tom coming in at all. When I was pretty sure there was no footage, I organised a sweep of the blind spots. There were loads of blind spots back then.

I sent Sam and Cherry from the front-desk team to do the stairwells, while I went to the canteen floor, which Tom said she had been looking forward to seeing. She wasn't there. I knew she wasn't there, but I kept looking. I went everywhere. All the places where we don't have any cameras.

The most likely looked to be the service racks on the third floor where Tom worked. Where she was last seen. He said he'd turned around and she vanished. So, it made sense that maybe she went through the side door – there were side doors, you see, built into the panels in the walls. This was so service operations could continue to function without disturbing the floors of workers. All the rubbish, all the hand sanitiser and all of that, was moved along in these service corridors.

They weren't hidden exactly, but they blended in, you could find them if you were looking, but you wouldn't notice if you were just going about your business as a worker on those floors. The toilets on every floor were connected by these corridors, as were a series of other maintenance access points. Fixing the air con, rebooting the power to the Wi-Fi units after a surge, it all got done through the access tunnels. If I was a young kid again, that's exactly where I would've gone.

I accessed the maintenance area on floor three, which had some of the oldest and most basic service corridors. I don't mind telling you, that place gives me the willies. It was concrete under foot, damp shuffle sound as you walk, which is more like a cave than a modern office building. The worst was the lighting.

Service lamps, placed at head height, running on a rail on just one side. You feel like you're walking in the dark, and someone else, someone you can't see, is blasting one side of your face with a flashlight. Nothing is lit except your face. It's blinding, absolutely blinding.

I held out my phone in front of me to try and balance out the glare, but it made no difference. Best use for it was to try and at least show where I was walking. There were wires slooped out about the place, half a coil in the torchlight looked like a rat's tail.

About halfway along the corridor, I started to get a sinking feeling in my stomach. It didn't feel right. The concrete floor was damp in places, and the shadows of the wires continued to seem alive. I kept calling out 'Hen!' – that's what her name was, apparently. I wasn't sure so I alternated with 'Chicken!' and a couple of times I just said, 'Little girl!' It sounded wrong, like not really my voice. The acoustics are strange in there, and it was curving never-endingly around to the left. Which didn't make much sense for a rectangular footprint, but I have learnt not to second-guess buildings of this kind. I started to hear my voice strangely. I said Hen again, I said Chicken. What kind of fuckwit names did this man give his children? In a dark moment, I said Joan's name, and it fell to pieces on my lips. Her name out loud in that horrible place, it wasn't right. But I thought maybe her name would keep the girl company, if she was lost, if we weren't ever going to find her. My thoughts were becoming distorted in there.

The darkness of my shadow too was wrong, I looked like a puppet. With the corridor's endless curve, I started to think I was going in a circuit of some kind. And then the lights went out – they're meant to be on a motion detector, you see, and from time to time the sensors fail, and you're left in darkness.

It wasn't much worse, really. I still had my phone, but I was no longer able to identify where I was along the corridor.

I started minding out for slits of light, I was sure I had covered all the ground I needed to. There was no possible way a little girl would have continued this far into the dark, I was sure of it, but there were no strips of light. No fluorescent markings to show a handle, no faint red LED that would denote life. I felt my chest getting tighter, and I could hear muttering sounds. And all along I am saying chicken, hen, little girl. My breath seemed frozen in my throat, so I was croaking it. If I'd heard that as a kid, I would have run away.

After a time, my phone battery died thanks to overuse as a torch. This meant I could no longer see my feet or where I was walking.

I began to think of that girl somewhere else. And the possibilities. I realised there were hundreds, actually thousands, of people in these buildings every day. And how much do we know about any of them really? I started running. Up ahead I could finally see light. My chest was burning with the panic and when I reached the lights I saw a figure.

Too big to be the missing girl. A man, not a child, but at least I could ask – have you seen anyone? How do I get out of this corridor? And then I saw who it was and my bones turned to chalk.

I still can't stress enough how hard that day had already been, so it was inevitable, or it now seems like it was inevitable, that I was going to have some kind of episode. I was clearly under a lot of pressure, but he was there, as clearly as you are now.

Cliff Rose. My old manager. He'd retired years before. He moved to Tenerife, but he was there all the same, he was perched on a high metal bench that stuck out of the wall – the same height as the row of lights. His legs dangled like a child's. I stood and talked to him.

'Cliff?' I said. 'How are you here?'

He said something about being called in for a meeting, but his face seemed not to see me directly. He was very tanned, looked like he was looking out to sea.

'How's Joan?' he asked me. That's my wife, Joan. They met a few times. When we used to have a Christmas do at ours – the 18th of December every year. Cliff'd come along with a bottle of Scotch under one arm, something for the kids in his other, and flowers with mistletoe in a bunch for Joan.

'Joan's all right,' I said. She had died after Cliff moved away. I didn't need to say she was dead. She was all right. Not alive, but all right. I don't know why I spoke to him. I suppose I knew it was just a vision, but I didn't mind. I went along with it. I knew it wasn't real.

'She's still making things out of wicker?' he asked.

'Yes, Cliff. She still does that. Although less than before.'

I felt like I had to give him something – he looked very sad to be sitting there all by himself in the dark, with his eyes still out to sea, so I carried on talking to him about Joan, talking as if she was still alive.

'Have you seen a girl come this way?' I asked him after a while. In a sort of lull in the conversation.

'No, haven't seen her, sorry Steve.'

I should have moved on at that point. Time had passed, I was sure quite a lot of time, especially if you include looking at all the CCTV footage, which had been a waste, I realised then, a waste of time. But I couldn't get away from Cliff. His legs were dangling. I'd not noticed before how small his feet were, and how short his legs. Could see the ghostly shape of his ankles too between his socks and his trousers. It was wrong for him to be there, but he continued to allude to some meetings he had been asked to attend, without addressing the fact that even if that was true, it didn't explain how he came to be here in a service corridor perched on the racking for the maintenance lights.

'I've got to find this girl, Cliff,' I said.

'She won't be found,' he replied; he seemed to be squinting into the sun. 'A missing person burns slowly. Like a sickness, but sped up. You start off being given this reason to worry, but it's probably nothing. She'll come back. Probably just got lost somewhere in the canteen. Sounds just like, it's only a lump, probably benign. You have this strong feeling that it will all be all right. You think you can just change your diet. And then gradually the tests come in and the feeling gets worse. You have more and more serious conversations. It's collective. You feel it together, the doctors guide you to the end. Same when someone's missing. You think they'll just be round the corner. They've hidden in the toilet. They've tailgated out of the building and gone home but it gets worse and worse. She isn't round the corner. She isn't in the garden. You start looking at cars.'

Cliff seemed to disconnect at that moment. I had this feeling that he was on a call or something but there was no way of seeing how he was connected to it.

I might as well mention that of course Joan thought she had IBS at first, when she was ill. She'd just been eating too much cheese when we were on holiday in France. Too much Camembert. Picked up a bit of bacteria. But a few weeks after we got back, things were getting worse instead of better.

It didn't take long – they said it had been there a long time, the cancer. She was happy, she said, that she hadn't known about it. I've survived it all this time without any worry. She smiled so much when she was dying.

'Still making basket cases!' Cliff said. 'Good old Joan.'

'I was her first one,' I said. 'Her biggest basket case anyway.'

'Her best,' said Cliff. The way his ledge, or whatever it was he perched on, was at the level of the work lights, he seemed animated. His face changed as one surface. 'You were her greatest basket case,' he said. It was a very un-Cliff thing to say. His voice was cracked, he sounded like he was on the radio. 'She's not with us any more,' he said. Almost whispering.

I didn't want to think about Joan any more in that tunnel. 'Cliff,' I said. 'I'm frightened of this situation. I'm worried because it's not real.' He waved me away; his hand was massive in the shadows, like an oar. It made me feel like I was being foolish. This was the first moment I considered that it might be real, what I was experiencing, because I had so little control over my feelings. I was completely under the spell of this apparition of Cliff.

'Where did you meet her again?' he asked. 'At the end of a party you threw, you told me.'

'It was someone else's party,' I said. 'But I'd rather not.'

'No please, please Steve, tell me, I want to know. Tell me.'

He looked terrified. His face swirling.

'All right. I have to be quick, this girl!'

'She won't be found.'

Jesus. So, anyway, I told him. 'Well it was a launch party, Cliff. Not someone's house, a launch party for a magazine that one of her friends was connected to. I was asked as a favour by the people running the bar for it. We were just working the door. All these wankers coming through all night, none of them on the guest list, all of them just waved through by the organisers. There was no need for security at all.'

'You bonded over the pointlessness of your job.'

'Just like us, Cliff.'

'It's freezing in here,' he said. 'It was cold that night, too?'

'It was the cold that brought us together. Both outside. Bloody waste of time.'

I glanced at Cliff again because he was making sounds like he was enjoying the conversation, but he kept looking out ahead of him. His breathing was incredibly shallow.

So I told him how I first fell in love with Joan. The party was over. People kept asking us to call taxis for them, and for some reason we did it. She organised a line and got in the road to hail them down. A makeshift rank. Drivers were on their radios telling others to come and get fares. We told them they're rich and cold and won't notice how much they pay. We saw these idiots off one car at a time. After an hour or more of this we were alone, no more people and also no more taxis. Powdery rain on the air, it was just us in the street – a fox moving about down the way. The sound of another screaming in a bush somewhere.

'It's freezing,' she said. Joan had this whisper she did when she was cold. She took a step towards me with her coat slightly open. I moved closer and she wrapped her coat around us both. It was a small coat, a leather jacket. We were there like that for a second, her face too close to see, and I try to remember what it was like the first time that happened. It's strange, trying to imagine being close to her for the first time. I still don't know now, though I've racked my brain for it, how it felt. I remember the smell of her leather jacket in the cold air. I remember the sharp smell of cigarettes late at night. I can't remember if she had her smell then, the one I came to know, and that seemed to change as we aged. I don't know. It pains me a great deal that I don't remember it well enough.

Anyway, there I was, in her coat, with my mind blank I suppose from the long night, and the cold.

I knew, I must have known, that something significant was

about to happen. It seems impossible to me now that I wouldn't have known.

She kissed me and that was it, the first time I fell in love with my Joan. Pretty boring, I suppose. Pretty basic. We didn't have any obstacles. We had been just young people in the city, and suddenly we were *connected*. Doosh! I went on to fall in love with her again, too. All the time, repeatedly, I fell in love with my Joan.

The next morning was the second time. I woke up and the radio was on. We were in her bedroom. Light came in through these thin curtains that seemed to go up forever. I could hear her voice speaking quietly, and realised she was calling in sick for her day job.

I sent a text to my line manager, also to say I was sick and sorry etc I won't be there. I fell in love with the space of her, the warmth on her side of the bed. This is it, I remember saying to myself. This is really it.

Cliff was listening the whole time. I had never talked to him like this before. He was smiling; that's wonderful, he said at one point. Quietly, as though he wasn't listening, but holding something precious in his hands. Wonderful.

I'll be honest, it almost felt like a disappointment when I realised what had happened when I met Joan. This was the person I knew I would spend the rest of my life with. All the other possible people vanished. I could almost see them, the other futures, looking at me sadly from the windows of a street. They held me in their gaze until I had walked underneath their windows and could not look back.

I grieved, I suppose. I felt sorry for myself. Isn't that stupid? But I was stupid, a complete moron.

If you've ever felt this way, this happy sadness on meeting someone, I strongly advise that you do not try and explain it to them. I never managed to show Joan the romantic side of it.

'I'll only ever love you now, isn't that amazing?' I said. 'But also . . .'

'But also what?' she asked.

Believe me, you don't want to get into it.

Then I fell in love with her again for some reason in a garden centre. For a whole year I felt it come on almost every weekend. I'd be holding a cup of coffee and she'd be reading a magazine in the sunlight, and I'd be almost in tears. There'd've been music, of course. Music always does it. I shiver.

Cliff shook his head. He called me a daft sod. Give her my love, he said. And he slid down from his perch and went off into the corridor.

I touched my face, which was soaked. I blew my nose and noticed a slice of cold fluorescent light up ahead. By the time I found my way back to my desk at reception, the search had been called off. I found my cover for the night, Selma, looking furious in the service office.

'This guy's daughter had never even *been* here!' she said.

'What do you mean, Selma?' I said.

'This guy, Tom. This *idiota*! They said he'd experienced an episode of some kind. He'd imagined the whole thing!'

'She's been found?' I asked. I didn't really understand what was happening.

'No! Not found because she never went missing. She's been at school all day. Can you believe it?! I've wasted most of the day looking for someone who isn't even there.'

I drank my cup of tea and didn't say anything.

Selma was meant to take the night shift, but she said that after all that business, she was sick. She wanted to get home and be with her kids. It was fair enough.

'I'll stay on, Selma,' I said.

That was the first night I stayed over in Capmeadow. I liked it – they gave me a sleep pod. Though I stayed away from the third floor.

I stayed another couple of nights after that in the pod, but then the hotel opened in the conference centre, so I was able to stay there. Your HR friends were glad I could do this. I had a meeting; you should have a record of it. Well, anyway, they only mentioned it to me once. 'You don't mind being in, Steve?' your colleague said. 'You don't need to get home?'

'What do I have to go back home to?' That's what I said. And you know what? That HR colleague nodded, like he understood, and I knew then that he had read the whole file on me. Widower. Always takes overtime. Probably has a bag ready in case he ever wants to just pick up and go, a bag with cash and his passport and a few clothes, a burner phone. I even had that, a phone that I could use but nobody knew about. All of these things for an escape into another life when this one became unbearable. Yes, he knew me.

'We have a place for you,' he told me. 'In the new expansion.'

Obviously, I never leave at all now. And that's why I think I deserve a chalet in the next allocation. I'm already a long-standing resident here – I don't know how long it's been, but I have seen many phases. And besides, you don't want me in the hotel any more. I must be costing you lot a fortune.

Tom Crowley: A sort of lament

They called my family; did you know that? I gave no such consent. It happened while I temporarily attended the all-hands town hall.

They said afterwards that they hadn't been able to find me, so they had reached out to my emergency contact. I don't understand how they could claim not to know where I was. I explained that I had to attend the town hall. Hen would be safe, I felt sure of it, and I felt sure that someone would come and get me. How did I feel sure that someone would come and get me? Because I asked both Jo from the office and Carl from the ops team to come and find me as soon as they laid eyes on Hen. I had all the apps open on my phone. I had to attend. I can't explain why, but I had to. The same way a smoker has to smoke, I had to be there.

Everyone in the support and ops teams had pictures of Hen.

So I was in a chair quite near the door. There was this joke that the CEO told, I don't remember what it was exactly, alluding to job losses, and I remember the room went silent as she berated her colleague, and I don't know if this was how everyone else felt, but it was quite extreme, like bullying almost.

His name was Vic or something. She was criticising him for the way the invitation email had made the announcement sound like it was going to be a big round of redundancies.

But of course it wasn't about that. And all the time she was talking, all I could think of was Hen, and the fact she was missing. She was missing. In the dark I had this hideous lurch in my stomach, what am I doing here? I was saying, what the fuck – actually mouthing these words, but not letting any sound out – what the hell am I doing sitting in this chair? I found myself doing this with my hand, little crab claw, we call it. I do this to remind myself of where she is and to somehow tell her that I'm thinking of her. I still do it, of course, more than ever. All this time – every day.

And of course, all along, while I was panicking, Hen was at school. She was at school all along. She was in her lessons, not trapped in a duct somewhere. She was fine. Fine fine.

I acknowledge it, I have gone on record acknowledging it. I accept that there is no evidence of her ever having been in the building. I helped with the HR report and the incident report and the Capmeadow business park safety report. I told them that I had believed completely that she was in the building, that I had taken a train with her, but that I must have been mistaken.

I was taken into a briefing room and shown videos of the train station where I walked, apparently alone, through the security gates.

'This is just for your peace of mind,' I was told. 'And for us to make absolutely sure nothing was done to you on that trip that could cause these false memories.'

I bristled a bit at 'false memories' but I had to admit that's what they were. I did not mention in this meeting how my body, my physical body still felt her loss. How it ached. I just confirmed that I had been dreadfully mistaken, and I was sorry, and I was happy to take steps to ensure I was fully able to return to work.

But my blood itched from it, the missing. She was missing. My Hen was gone. She was there, of course, and the girl I would go on to pick up from school, who I would tuck in that night, who would make me laugh like always, I was careful, so careful, not to fall short of loving her. But my daughter, still, all the same, was gone.

I felt the two things equally, the gladness of a parent to be assured of the safety of their child, and the broken dust-blown desolation of bereavement. So, of course, while I accepted the premise that Hen was safe, had never come on the train with me, was enjoying her day at school, also I opened my eyes as wide as I could when I turned to the screen in the briefing room, determined to absorb every single pixel of the footage of me arriving at the station, hunting the greyness for a sign of my daughter.

'Here we are again, Mister Crowley,' the security manager said. He was not an unkind man; he was soft all over his features. You wouldn't credit him with the kind of heft required for security work, until you considered the size of him. He was vastly tall, with arms like an albatross. He smelled of sweat coming through pure clean skin.

'There you are, look. Alone.'

'I think she was behind me by quite a way at that point,' I said. 'In my false memory.'

The security manager was very calm about this. 'That's OK, we can keep it running.'

'She was quite a way behind me.'

He smiled. 'We have five hours of footage. How far behind could she have been?'

I watched the gate at the train station with my breath held.

I asked them to rewind it a few times to double-check that it really was me coming through the turnstile. I had never been confronted with the way that I walk from that angle.

'I look like I'm with her,' I said. Nobody responded to this. The security manager seemed to smile, but it was too quick for me to really notice it. 'I look harassed, look. She was acting up on the train. I shouted at her.' My throat tightened as I said this. A vast wave of guilt hit me again. I watched in silence for a few more seconds. Far longer than she could have credibly been behind me if she had been there.

'This is definitely from the right date?' I asked again.

'Yes, see for yourself.'

The date and time were in the corner of the video.

'Could that be wrong?'

'No.'

I went on watching, became almost hypnotised, the people seemed to be moving in a pattern. I started counting, looking for flickers in the screen, repeated shifts in the background. I felt sure I saw the same guy go through the gates with his bike multiple times.

'Look,' I said. 'You see? It's a pattern. There's something wrong with this footage.'

'They're different guys,' said the security manager. 'See, different jacket.'

The security manager was right. The cyclist had a different jacket each time he went through the barrier. Of course, they weren't just different jackets, but different people, but I still thought of it as the same man over and over again. And it looked like a pattern because they were all behaving in the same basic way. They walked strangely, to me, they walked as though they were not individually motivated to walk, but were programmed to do so.

I didn't speak this thought out loud. This was what people I work with would call a gotcha moment. I was being shown this irrefutable evidence that my daughter was never here. As though seeing her, talking to her, holding her was not already irrefutable. And yet I refuted it.

'Could she, possibly, do you think, have gone through without being seen by the camera?' I said.

'No mate, I'm sorry, but it's not possible.'

'It's so weird. I need to sit down I think.'

'You're already sitting down, mate.'

That smile again from the security manager. I never saw him again after that meeting. This story is full of people I only met once. I'm sorry about that. Have you noticed? How many people come through here. Like through that barrier, almost without faces, without any heft to them at all. I felt suddenly responsible for so many people wasting their time. The people through the barriers too, somehow I felt bad for making them go through over and over again to satisfy something in me which had clearly broken.

'I'm sorry,' I said at some point. Just to fill the air. To let them know.

'Don't worry, mate. It's weird isn't it?' the security manager said. 'It's hard to get used to watching people on these tapes. It looks like a computer program at first. The way they move . . .'

'It's fine, really,' I said. 'I feel stupid. OK, there is a clump of people who come through about thirteen seconds after me. Can we rewind it again? I think if we can rule that out one more time, I think we're done.'

He rewound the tape again. I liked him, he showed no sign at all of being tired of having to go through all this with me.

'I feel like I'm losing my mind,' I said. I must have said this a thousand times, just in that one meeting.

'She's safe,' the security manager repeated. 'That's what matters. All we're doing now is double-checking. This is for you, so whatever you need.'

If you're thinking this all seems like a lot of effort for Capmeadow's security team to go through, well, I agree. And I wasn't going to say anything at the time, but I found that single fact alone to be of extreme interest. What are they looking for on these videos? I wondered. How did they get hold of the footage at all? Surely it's not the sort of thing that a train company or whatever hands out?

'By the way,' I said. 'I haven't seen this room before. Is it new?'

'Part of the expansion,' the security manager said.

'I feel like this is underneath the old car park,' I said.

'No – take a look.'

The security manager opened the curtain and I saw that we were at least seven or eight floors up. I could see buildings A and B in the distance. Between here and there several low-rise buildings, hulking sports centres, the spiralling tower of Capmeadow Hotel.

'It's astonishing,' I said.

'Just watch the tape, please. We do need to close this work out today.'

I went back to watching again. Again I asked it to be rewound. Again the security manager agreed.

'It jumped!' I said while we watched, minutes after I had passed through the gate. 'Just then? Did you see it skip? It skipped, I'm sure of it. Is there some footage missing?'

'No, it didn't skip,' he said. 'The clock is constant, no skip.'

We sat in silence again, watching the movement on the screen as it became less and less real to me.

'Did you ask your neighbours and friends like we suggested?' he asked.

'Yeah. None of them saw Hen.'

I had been told that I was seen heading to the station alone by three people on our street, and apparently by the owner of the shop on the corner, and the early butchers at Golden Meat who were taking a cigarette break after their breakfast. The footage finished for the final time.

I accepted it. I signed the forms. I apologised.

'Will I lose my job?' I asked.

'This is not the time to worry about such things,' said the HR contact, who was with us now in the room. I had not heard him enter, but no sooner had he spoken than the air around us became completely infused with his perfume. The guy went everywhere in a tent of it. I liked his perfume against my will, and it was the same with him.

'You might need some time off,' he said. 'The company is here to support you.'

'When can I come back then?' I tried not to sound too desperate, because I didn't want them to get the idea that I still thought I would find her somewhere in the office. Of course I wouldn't, but the vastness of the place staggered me. When had this enormous growth happened? And most of all, I thought, she is out there without me. She is alone. I felt completely paralysed.

'We will monitor it all,' said the HR partner. 'Please don't worry about it for now.'

I remember him now. I wonder if he still works here, the HR partner I met with. He smiled before everything he said. Was his name Giovanni? It was something like that. A name from a place that he himself was clearly not from.

'At the moment,' he said, 'focus on getting better, yes? You will receive your full salary for up to six weeks, and then we will assess the situation.'

I started to say that there was too much to do, I wasn't sure I could take any time off, I even started listing my training design tasks about which he obviously knew nothing and cared even less. He grabbed hold of my wrists, holding me loosely, but with an unnecessary sense of urgency. He stared into my eyes, which was embarrassing. He acted like I was having a seizure.

'OK, look at me, Tom. Look at me. You have to focus on yourself, yes? Work can wait, yeah? We will find a way.'

I was about to assure him that I would be fine, that I'd admitted I knew my daughter hadn't gone missing. Something had happened, that's all. I would be fine, but someone was coughing suddenly. I thought it was the security manager, but he had gone. I hadn't heard him leave. The coughing started in the dark corner of the room. Someone else was with us, barely visible in the dark corner. Had they been there the whole time? Hiding in the shadows. Even coughing, this person was very low impact. They made virtually no impression on the room. They wore glasses. There was no introduction.

Nobody spoke while the unseen person continued to cough. I guess they weren't meant to draw attention to themselves, whoever they were.

I remember they managed to say, 'Excuse me,' but only after a good half a minute of rattling away. They didn't step into the light and get a glass of water from the table. Also, I now recall, I didn't offer to help by getting them one. I don't suppose it's possible now to find out who that was.

I went on sick leave for six weeks, but I actually had to work for a lot of that time, supporting the Capmeadow expansion training effort. I had to write warning signs – a lot of signage text saying things like 'Difficult walkway' and 'Immature lake' – without knowing why, or what was

BEN PESTER

happening to cause such hazards.* I was here more than ever, is the reality.

I left the meeting room, still with the sense that I was surrounded by teeming pixelations of people rushing past me. The figure I had been on the video was upsetting. Who is this tense man? What do my children see?

All I wanted was to hold my daughter's hand. I wanted to walk with her and tell her how funny my day had been. I looked for you on a video, but you weren't there, I would say. And then tell her the whole stupid story. Even thinking about it put a lump in my throat.

But another feeling was creeping through already, poisoning the normally beautiful sense of anticipation I would feel when I was going to see my children and had a story to tell them. The sense that this whole event should never be mentioned to her.

There was a clear risk it could be mistaken for probing. I was already getting the idea that something was breaking down in my marriage, something was at risk, and if I started talking this madness to our daughter, it would get worse. I worried that by making light of it, I would look like I was probing her mind to find out if she remembers going missing. If it is a shared hallucination. Of course, I would never do this. If you think about it for a second, imagine pushing a child to share in your delusions. I shouldn't indulge it, that seemed to be the way to move forward. And so, yes, I readjusted my outlook.

*

---

* **Archivist's note:** We now believe these immature lakes were early ancestors of our physical data reservoirs. It's not clear if Tom would have seen them.

As I made my way to the main exit after the meeting, I saw a few people I recognised, not by name, but well enough for us to nod a hello to each other. I tried to gauge their reactions as I passed them by.

I found myself in the road, in a call with another HR rep. This one told me her name, but I am ashamed to say it didn't stay with me. So often, I am talking to people and I have no idea who they are really. I am so sorry for this.

'You need to see a doctor,' she was saying. Her voice was cutting through all other sound. I could just about hear her, but I couldn't hear anything else. 'Your appointment is in the Green Area on floor thirty-five.'

'But I've left,' I said. 'I'm walking towards the train station.'

'Hmm,' she said.

I looked around me to find that the trees and Victorian houses were not there. The streets you have to walk through to get from the Capmeadow site had given way to more Capmeadow. I was actually just in the car park.

'Never mind,' I said. 'I've walked in a loop or something. Actually a doctor sounds like a good idea.'

'She's expecting you. No need to wait, just go straight in. Green Area, floor thirty-five.'

I had expected to get lost, but I found the Green Area on floor thirty-five pretty easily. I saw a few people I didn't recognise milling around. There was a general sense of confusion on the faces of most of the people I saw.

'I had to walk miles,' a woman was saying. 'Has it always been this far?'

She was accompanied by a much brighter, happier colleague who smiled and shook her head in sympathy.

The two women vanished out of sight. I didn't see where they went.

The Green Area was called that, I guessed, because the floor was green, and there were many hanging planters with pearlish succulents cascading down, and trough planters with foliage peeping out, and large – like the size of a small car – pots with mature tropical plants in them. Enormous leaves and the sound of water babbling. I could not see a single wall. Signs for the surgery were painted on the floor.

There was no door. I got to the waiting room through a series of turnings that led to a less and less green space, and more and more white space. There were a lot of people in there. It looked like a normal doctor's surgery.

[A voice: Are you able to expand on what you mean by a normal doctor's surgery?]

Non-office people were in there. There was a man who had obviously had an accident of some kind doing manual work, he was holding an ice pack against his head. A child with pale grey skin with his mother. Must have been about three years old, looking very under the weather.

Obviously this could all still mean they were colleagues or the children of colleagues, but there were no office workers, from what I could see. It just felt like a normal community practice.

I asked at the reception desk the way to the doctor's room. I gave my name.

'She's expecting you,' the receptionist said.

I was shown round another series of walls, like the lane dividers they have for long queues, but instead of ropes they were full white plaster walls.

The doctor knew who I was. She acted as though she had been my personal GP for years. She made me feel at home. Had someone bring me a cup of tea. We sat in silence for a while. I didn't really know what I was there for.

'Do you need to run some tests?' I said.

'What for?'

'Um, to see if there's something wrong with my brain?'

'Do you think there's something wrong with your brain?'

'No.'

'Here, squeeze this,' the doctor said, suddenly handing me this thing. I squeezed it. A kind of leather egg with beads in it.

'Again.'

I squeezed it again.

'Again.'

I squeezed it again. Then she nodded and took it away from me.

'Would you like to tell me what happened?'

'I thought I had lost my daughter in the office,' I said. 'But it turns out she has been at school the whole time.'

The doctor looked at me as though what I'd said was completely normal.

'Have you spoken to her yet?' she asked.

'Not yet. I was on my way home, but they told me to come here. I just want to see her. I got so stressed and cross with her on the train. But, of course, I can't have got cross because . . .'

'Because she wasn't on the train. I understand. Do you want to tell me what you remember from this morning?'

I told her the whole story from the moment I left the house, just as I've told you. My voice shook, and I was nervous, just as my voice shakes now, just as I am nervous now of course, and, by the way, I must apologise if this constant up and down, looking away and looking back is strange. I feel that even though I have my notes, even though I have been through this countless times as I built up the courage to come and talk to you, even though I have prepared, I feel unable to stop looking and looking away. I feel worried that I have been changed by all of this.

[**A voice: Please don't worry. You're doing very well. You were saying about the doctor . . .**]

Yes, the doctor. I told her everything. She nodded slowly and then, although she didn't mean for me to see it, she glanced at the clock.

'It was a nasty shock,' she said eventually. 'Spend time with the family, your feelings will settle. The mind is strange,' she said. 'The body is strange.'

She looked at the clock again, more overtly, then she moved her chair forward and began typing, talking to me but looking at the screen.

'Your mind thinks your daughter vanished,' she said. 'So it has a memory of it happening. But she didn't vanish. As you know. You do know that, don't you?'

'Yes. Of course,' I said, barely keeping the words in the correct shape. I'd said over and over again that of course I had been mistaken, but this time it felt wrong, it felt jagged on the mouth, like I was denying her existence. She had been there. I was sure she had been there.

'Take a breath. Then say it again.'

I took a breath. 'I know she wasn't there. I know she wasn't there.'

'You're sure?'

'I know she wasn't there.'

'Good. That's the main thing. The sooner you're back into a healthy routine that includes some self-care, the sooner your brain will stop using that memory – the memory of taking your daughter to work – and the cells that hold that information will be allowed to die away. Soon the day you didn't take your daughter to the office will be more like a memory of a dream. If you remember it at all.'

'I keep looking for her,' I said. 'Out of the corner of my eye, I keep thinking I can see her.'

'No, you can't see her. She's not here. Did they show you the footage from the train station?'

'They did.'

'Stop looking for her. Here, hold this.'

The leather egg again. I held it.

'Stop looking for her,' the doctor said. 'She is exactly where she's meant to be. Squeeze.'

I squeezed.

'Again.'

I squeezed again.

'Good.'

In one movement, the doctor took the leather egg away from me, stood up and moved to the door.

'You'll be fine,' she said. 'Stick to your routines, spend time with her. Do not look for her in the workplace or anywhere else. I have written to your manager already with your sick note. I have said that you can do some light duties as you are part of something important that they tell me is called the Capmeadow expansion project. Otherwise, you are to relax. Spend time with your daughter,' she said.

'Do I need any medication for my mood, do you think?'

'No,' she said, holding the door open. 'What's wrong with your mood?'

'I don't know. I feel strung out.'

'I think if you didn't feel strung out after your experiences in the last few hours, then you'd really have a problem. Get some rest. It will pass.'

'But what if it doesn't?' I said. 'Do you think I have had a problem for a long time? Don't you think it's worth checking?'

She continued to hold the door open. She looked at me, she looked back at the clock.

'Why do you keep looking at the clock?' I said, rather offended and getting red in the face again. 'Am I getting in your way?' I could feel my heart accelerating, a sourness coming on. I took a breath, I tried to smile or at least look as pleasant as I could. I probably did not look pleasant.

The doctor remained by the door. She showed no emotion on her face. 'Mr Crowley,' she said. 'What I really think is that you're incredibly busy and very tired. In fact, I *have* been check-ing the clock. I have been checking the clock because I know you have to get to the school to collect your daughter.'

'Oh.'

'I think it's essential that you get there on time. Do you agree?'

'Yes, I agree.'

'Right, so, I will let you be on your way.'

I left, and followed the signs to the exit. Once I was back in the waiting room, I went to the receptionist's desk to ask if I needed to come back in for a further consultation and was told I could leave. I felt sure I could hear someone asking me about my recent workload, specifically how available I was for new projects. The waiting room was completely empty.

The light faded as I walked from the train station to Hen's school. There was no colour except this unbearable blind-ing gold that seemed to touch everything and then die away. The trees in the park rattled. It felt like I would never get to the school on time. By the time I got to the gate, I was not in what you would call a good condition.

I felt my knees give as I trod on spongy areas on the playground surface. There were these divots all over the place left over from old climbing frames. Replacements were always placed in some new spot, so the whole playground was potted with air pockets. The experience of walking over them was like the feeling of a grave underfoot.

The cold was insufferable. I shivered, felt completely skinless, but nobody else seemed to notice. The other parents were in shirts with small knitted jumpers over the top and seemed fine.

The top-earning fathers of my daughter's class had their sleeves rolled up, forearms with brutal quantities of hair, heavy watches. Their dark chinos tight across their arses, which seemed to be swollen like bee allergies. Others were wearing sportswear cowls that fluttered in the breeze. They all had a calmness for parenting, I always thought. A natural gentleness I lack. One of them came to talk to me.

'All right, Tom!' It was Aidan or Andrew or Drew or something like that. His kid – his older kid – had been in my son's year when he attended this school. His son did not go on to the same secondary school as mine. I doubt they were even in touch any more by this time.

'Hiya,' I said.

'You all right, mate? You look a bit peaky.'

I didn't know how to respond. I was still staring at the exit, waiting for Hen. Waiting for her to exist. I felt like seeing her would give me a heart attack.

'I'm fine, fine thanks,' I mumbled. 'I've er, been in a hot room.'

'A hot room is it?' Aidan or whatever laughed at that like it was an innuendo, but it wasn't an innuendo. This fucking guy.

I was pretty sure it had been one of his kids involved in picking on my son a few years earlier.

'Ha, no, I mean, you know, working from home. Heating's on. I come out and the whole world is freezing.'

'Oh right, yeah.' We stood there like this for a bit longer. I could smell him now, I remembered that smell. And the more I could smell it, the more he reminded me of that shit with my son. A couple of bigger kids in his class – one of them, I was now convinced, definitely Aidan or Andrew or Drew's son. Whatever his fucking name was. They'd been following my boy to the toilet, waiting until he was inside a cubicle, and then kicking the end wall of the stalls which caused all the doors to open. He always needed time on the toilet, you know. He couldn't understand why they would do this.

It took us three weeks to get him to tell us that this was why his pants often had horrible stains in them, because he was too scared to be in there long enough to wipe himself. He was too scared to go at all. The shame of him admitting it, the anger in our voices, clumsy, desperate for him to just tell us so we could fix it. Unbearable, his tiny frame, the smell. I remember being so angry, I wanted to burn the school down. But I couldn't and I couldn't get the names of the kids out of him, and we didn't know what to do. It was devastating waiting to see his little face, pinched, unhappy and unable to speak about it. Do you know, even today I still remember this moment when I join him on a video call, I wait to see his face, I wait to see the marks that have been left there by the treatment he receives from others.

He works now, of course, is out there, in a leadership role somewhere, I expect. Or if not, then probably leading in some way.

I receive text messages from him like jewels mined out of rock. I'm sorry, he says, it has been a very long time. It has been a very long time since I saw him. Have you seen him? Of course no, no you wouldn't have.*

This problem – my son's problem, I mean, with those boys – had gone away without my doing anything – which was lucky, because I was completely powerless. I wanted to burn the school down, which, when I said it out loud in the kitchen to Eliane, my wife, made my son cry, and I had to go out for a walk in the fresh air.

With Hen, there had been no such problems with other kids. She seemed invincible. There was nobody who didn't know her, nobody who had a pet she didn't know the name of. I was jealous of her recall for names and faces, her enthusiasm for other people's lives. She seemed able to devour them like books. And yet, I could never shake the feeling that some of my awkwardness had been passed on to her. Some of this incapacity I have, like anger, and failure, always there beneath the surface. Does everyone have that? When I looked at her I'd worry that they don't, and that I'm not normal, and I have passed on this abnormality to her.

---

* **Archivist's note:** Time anomaly here. Perhaps Thomas misspoke? Otherwise it raises the question of how many months or years have passed between him losing (or not losing) his daughter. Massive questions about the age of Capmeadow records arising here. And deeper in.

Also – in the background, while he specifically refers to his now-adult son (who was school age during his first exposure to Capmeadow's expansion), there are strange interfering sounds:

There is the sound of someone pouring and drinking a glass of water. Then refilling and drinking again, and one further time. There is the sound of breathing. I can hear the sound of breathing even with my headphones off, which I have noted here but will delete soon. I'm not sure what the breathing sound was, but it has stopped now.

For all her abilities in the general bustle of life, I have felt uneasy watching her in smaller groups. In a pair, she seemed lost. Did they like her enough? Did they get it? Was she able to engage?

'Well, here they come anyway,' I said. I realised Aidan had already moved away. I looked around for him, but he'd faded into the rows of other dads.

Hen was coming out. Her class finally emerged in a clipped military line. For a split second I thought she wasn't going to be there. The ground started to open up, and then it was OK. Hen was at the back of the line; she looked the same as always from that distance. It was the same walk as ever. Same everything. She saw me and I waved. The same exact wave. Everything was the same. My body reacted the same way it always did. A fullness suddenly, a small and regular display of balloons in the stomach, in the lungs, the air sweetened. I waved at her teacher to acknowledge that I was here to take her home, and Hen was released. She charged towards me and leapt. I held her tight and breathed her in. It was real, her voice, her sound, the smell of her clothes and her end-of-day breath, it was all completely real. Only, I could not see her face.

I kissed her cheek, put her down, tried to look at her, and could not properly see her face.

'Take your hood off, chicken!' I said.

She removed her hood, but a sweep of hair still frayed across her eyes. She kept moving her head somehow, not wildly, but something about it meant I couldn't see her – not all of her face at the same time. I stepped back, her face shrank out of focus into the neck of her puffer jacket. She started to walk away from me and I dashed to keep up, holding her hand and slowing her.

'Was school good?' I said. A little too breathless, a little too behind her still.

'Yes, Daddy.'

'You had fun.'

'Yes!'

We smiled at each other. I thought we did, I couldn't tell completely. Her mouth was smiling, then her eyes were smiling, but I couldn't see them together. I gave her a high five. Everything was fine, I told myself. Everything is exactly as it should be. As we walked, she seemed to flicker at my side.

'We've got chips for tea,' I said. It wasn't true until I said it. Chips, chips for tea. Fine, why not? Where is your face, I was thinking. Is that you?

'OK.'

We kept walking. The park again was cold, the vicious trees. At some point in this walk I felt the swell of a meeting room.

'The doctor told me I have to go away for a while,' I said.

'OK, Daddy.'

A voice speaks at length

First of all, I want to say thank you again for seeing me today. I hope you actually can see me. There have been a few of these meetings now and I am not sure if you're there live, or if you catch up on a recording. Sometimes I wonder if you are over there at all, in the darkness, but it doesn't matter. Just to be able to speak and feel heard. That's what matters. Perhaps, if you are here in the room with me, if you feel able to, perhaps sometime we could both be in the light. It's not so bad once your eyes get used to it. But then maybe it would break the spell of this. I do need to speak. If I could see your face, and ask who you are, or maybe not who you are, but I suppose I would have other questions. They would distract me. I can see that this is somehow a method. I approve of the method. I wish you well always. I will start now.

I am blessed to have such a supportive work environment. I made myself a promise to speak with conviction and honesty, and to leave wallowing and self-pity at the door. I think it's so important to state the facts and let the emotional side of things run its course, but not fan the flames.

I'd like to start by describing my daily meetings. As I have mentioned before, these are the bulk of my working day at the moment. I have a more strategic focus in my job title, and job description of course, but right now, I'm needed to host the feedback sessions and break everything down into the correct data. I think it says on the agenda for this meeting that I should give you a full rundown of how my meetings have been going, and more specifically of how I structure the dialogue.

So, I normally thank the guest for coming to see me – I do this before I offer any refreshment. I want them to feel positive about this experience from the second they come in, so I thank them for even making the time to come here. I say, it's really great for us to get feedback about the new developments at Capmeadow. Your time is so valuable, I say. And then I offer a drink and snacks. Normally people just have water, but sometimes they want tea. Biscuits are provided but rarely taken. I have a lot of unused biscuits to give to my team at the end of most days.

I know things really move fast in the Capmeadow expansion project; I say that next, and I emphasise that sometimes it can be overwhelming. And at this point, I gesture or somehow otherwise prompt the visitor to take over the talking. Sometimes I have to say, don't you agree? But usually not. They are very keen to get on with their side of it.

Saying 'things can be overwhelming' is a great way to end the intro, I find – I don't have any specific examples for them, because either it is overwhelming and they tell me why, or it isn't overwhelming and I let them explain why it's actually not overwhelming but something else. So many times, someone will say, 'Well, I'm not overwhelmed. I'm actually a bit cross . . .' and they go from there.

I don't have any boundaries in terms of what they can talk about. I mean, I don't tolerate abusive language directed at me, but when people swear for emphasis or out of frustration, then it's OK. I have a team who are there to support me when I have a situation that might be getting out of control. But ninety-nine per cent of the time, people speak respectfully about their issues and how we can resolve them.

In fact, a lot of the time, there really isn't an issue to be resolved in that sense. A lot of the time, they just want to talk to someone about how it feels to work somewhere like Capmeadow, and at the moment that someone is me.

Everyone is aware that what they say is encrypted. It's not confidential because the data is passed back to the company, as well as being fed into the Capmeadow records. But it's all anonymised. Only the person with the correct key can see it, and even then they cannot know whose key they have. And even then, it's data, not language at that point. You might as well slosh your hand into the data reservoirs and swirl them around. It's the exact same deal.*

There are some things that people are not permitted to talk to me about, but I do not know what those things are. I only know that they can't talk to me about them. Whenever they seem to be about to talk about something they are forbidden to mention (not *forbidden*, I apologise, this word has crept into my language recently and I think it's because one of my team used to work in the copywriting division; there has been a spread, only a mild one, of off-message language – so, not *forbidden* but *non-accepted*), something gently happens to move them back onto a more appropriate track. Certain topics cannot be discussed with me for data security and privacy reasons. There

---

* **Archivist's note:** I can hear this, I can almost hear it, the hand of this listener touching the coolant, swirling. It makes me feel like a great thirst is about to be quenched. But then nothing; no matter how many times I watch her talking, I reach for a glass of water at this point.

are counsellors and things like that for very personal issues. I am specifically here to handle Capmeadow estate and experience matters.

Very often there is positive feedback – I feel like not enough is said about that. There are a lot of people who feel good – I am trying to encourage them to come to me and talk about it so that my data is giving a more balanced picture. Or maybe knowing that only a few extra-motivated people have real problems is enough. I feel like the data is way more complex than anything I contribute, but I worry about it almost constantly. Is that bad? I should calm down maybe about the data. I suppose I only mention it now because it matters to me to know that this project is, overwhelmingly, a success. Capmeadow is proving us right time and again in terms of satisfaction and focus. My crew – Cath, Jay and Ed from the inbound architecture-growth services team – I'm sure you know about them – are incredibly enthusiastic about the new shopping experiences we have, and the guided walks through the newer landscaping have been nothing short of mesmerising.

I took my first guided walk with Amber, who I would like to spend more time with. (I feel like she understands this place better than anyone else I've met here. Sadly we haven't had time to catch up again since that walk, and I worry too about whether I said or did something to put her off.)

There was a moment when we strayed from the guided pathways and found ourselves at a limit of the expansion. I've seen it before, of course, the way the edges grow out, the way they glisten and have a slight odour, but Amber seemed momentarily stuck. Not disgusted, but a bit hypnotised. There is something, I suppose, *creeping* about the way the land map expands underfoot. The slime on the tiles, and so on. I like it. If you look closely, the way it reproduces itself is like breathing. A living community fabric.

'I don't think I wanted to see that,' Amber said. 'It makes me feel strange seeing it grow like that.'

I tried to tell her it was OK, non-toxic, etc. I advised her not to touch the unformed lip of the ground surface, like all the training material says, but I needn't have been so concerned. She wouldn't even go near it.

'I don't think I want to see this,' she said again. She looked completely white; her lips, I noticed, were very dry. 'I don't think I am supposed to be here,' she said. I was upset to hear this, I didn't think she had these problems too. But then, she had said 'supposed to be here', which was strange, because most people just say, 'I'm not actually here.'

Anyway.

I pulled her gently by the arm and we found our way back onto the guided path. We both had stand-up meetings at around that time, so we found a suitable stop-off to attend those. Afterwards, we completed a tour of some flowerbeds and returned to the shopping experiences. We had matcha hot chocolate with spices selected for us by the waiter.

'I enjoyed walking with you today, Amber,' I said.

So, I do take their views seriously, and I include my notes, of course, as I compile my research and feed it back into the data resource.

Mostly, they just need to speak.

Yesterday, for example, I heard from a co-worker who had been allocated living space in the Third New Region of Capmeadow – formerly called expansion C – and wanted to discuss some of the planting in the communal areas. She came into my office space in a distressed state – not unusual. She was tired, this colleague. She smelled of the mint pastilles that they sell in the some of the older coffee places. Nostalgic Aromas it might have been. Or Phil's. I got the feeling she ate quite a lot of the mint pastilles. She wanted to talk about some of the rapid changes to her accommodation.

'We went to bed, me and my partner, as normal,' she told me. 'I was having a dream, and he woke me up right in the middle of it. He was fidgeting. He said it was because he could smell insects. The smell of these insects woke him up!'

I was intrigued by this information. I asked her to explain what she meant.

'Stink bugs!' she said. She banged the table and glared at me. I'm sorry to say I did laugh at this outburst. I had never heard of them before. Did you know this? There's an insect we get now, a kind of cricket or something – she didn't describe it very well – that emits a strong fragrance. They think it arrived here stashed in the plants of the tropical wellness gardens that are a feature of the Capmeadow landscape.

It woke this woman's partner in the night and he got up and went off. She was asleep, as I have mentioned, and was in the midst of quite a deep-sounding dream.

'In the dream I am shutting a car door,' she said. 'I close the car door, and just as it hits, I am in the car and I can see my mother touching the door, having just closed it. And then I am driving the car, but when I look up, I am looking at the back of my mother's head. I never see anyone's face in the dream. Someone in the car says, oh look, I can see the sea. I was just about to look at the sea when he woke me up, struggling out of bed.'

He was gone for about three hours, because of the stink bugs. She says he came back resolved to end the relationship. He spent the night walking the limits of the Capmeadow estate, and came back different, that's what she said.

'He was shaking me in my bed!' she told me. 'It's wrong, he kept saying it's wrong. He kept saying that he had taken a wrong turn!'

She continued to say that her partner was now a stranger to her, and all, she said, as a result of the fragrant insects.

'What are you going to do about this smell?' she kept saying. 'He's moved to the other side of the business park. What am I supposed to do now? I had made so many plans.'

I couldn't say much, unfortunately. I obviously can't do anything about insects. Or about her partner's reaction to an insectile smell. I mean, where do you start with that?

Officially, I am not responsible for any kind of estate maintenance, and I have no influence over the residential contract each colleague has with the firm. These contracts evolve almost as fast as the space itself, which is completely normal, as I have to explain regularly.

I am simply here to listen, and I listen attentively to absolutely every issue. It's not much good if I start telling people, actually, that's got nothing to do with me. You'll have to take this problem to estates, because I know nothing will get resolved if I do that. The only way I can help is to listen and to present the data back to you, as I have been doing.

So I either stay silent until I can be of use, or I say that sounds very difficult. I then promise to action their problems. I say, thank you for telling me this. We will pass all of this along, so it will be logged. But of course, I'm just referring to the normal passing along of information. It doesn't necessarily mean anything will be done about it, or not directly, anyway. But I always listen with care, I can look them in the eye about that. I listen with care even though what they say often doesn't make any sense at all, and is not really fitting for a professional environment.

This is a workplace! I feel like I have to remind myself, and remember at all times, this is a workplace.

In the case of the insect smell, something *was actually done*, I think, because I got several reports saying thank you for ending that pervasive smell. A predator was introduced to control the smelly insect population. That was the solution. I was never informed as to the nature of this predator.

Between you and me, I was sad about that. I never got to smell this insect smell. I would have liked to, I think. It sounds like something I would recognise.

I don't have many really complete childhood memories, but I'm sure that we once went away on a camping holiday, and I remember hearing the sound of grasshoppers and crickets and cicadas for the first time. A chorus of all these different animals. It was astonishing, the sound never ended and it was impossible to see any reasonable source. But I never smelled them. There was no fragrance. I'd love to know what it smelled like. I'd love to know that.

The biggest thing that people want to talk about when they come and see me is change. It's constant here, obviously. We're in such an exciting phase of the expansion now.

For example, I myself live in the new second main district, and before that I was in the first phase accommodation. I've been here through every stage so I am familiar with the pace of change, but even I can still get disoriented.

For example, I went on a date with Robin recently. Do you know Robin Stone? I think he's the only one with that name. You probably can't confirm that. Your job is similar to mine – everything is confidential. Although, you have an even more elaborate working space than I do! What a space this is. How much it makes me relax and feel comfortable talking. Only Capmeadow would have something like this. It lifts the heart.

Anyway, I was saying about this date. I don't often go on dates, but I really wanted to try the new noodle place that had opened in the boundary sector, so I asked Robin if he wanted to come along.

It was just a friendly thing really, but he seemed flattered to have been asked, and I couldn't back-pedal enough to say it was just as friends. So we agreed to take it seriously as a date. We got dressed up, we met at the agreed time, he even brought me flowers, but he was bored after a while, I think. Or he was maybe upset by something. I couldn't work it out. At one point I worried that I was boring him, and the fact is I wished I was there with someone else. I wished I was with Amber, who I mentioned before. I kept thinking, Amber would have shared food with me. She would've already been saying amusing things. She would have held my arm and said, 'Why did they decide to have all those tubes coming out of the building?' She would have laughed at it. I would have been able to just say something like 'Tentacles!' and made movements like a monster. I was thinking this kind of thing the whole time Robin was talking. I tried to be light and enjoy the moment, but Robin felt so heavy. Another heaviness. I have enough heaviness. Maybe all of this is really unfair on him actually. Maybe I am treating a good guy badly by talking about this. I don't know – what do you think? I guess it started OK. I was glad we decided to meet under date-style conditions because even though I already knew nothing would happen, I liked the idea of being slightly nervous. I enjoyed thinking about it. I feel as though I have always been this way. With the pressure of work, with the expansion project in such an exciting and intense phase, sometimes I need to simplify everything. I take a small, tiny thing, and let that be my focus. I don't enlarge it, but I think, 'Let this occupy me.'

In a clean room, for example, I might place a sock on the floor so I have something to think about.

Noodles with Robin was like that. Go on the date, nothing will happen, but still I can sit and think the nothing for several days.

Robin is good-looking, or at least, I think so, up close. From a distance he is maybe a little chaotic, but he is good-looking in small details. The area between his eye and his ear when he looks down. His neck when he leans back in a chair. I mean good-looking here like a picture can be good-looking. He was like that, like a picture. But a sad one.

And he knows how to make an effort with his clothes and stuff like that. So I knew it would be OK to be with him – he would make an effort. We would match up well aesthetically, and he smells good. He has two fragrances that I've noticed and I like. A third one he wears I am much less fond of. But that is personal taste. Other people would say he always smells good.

One thing I did not expect was that he would be so un-focused. I don't work directly with him, but he seemed like he would be diligent and committed. I can't explain why, maybe because his clothing choices were so neat and clean. Mostly from his appearance, I admit, and from some general impressions I got over coffee, I expected him to be placid and to just enjoy things at face value.

You know what I mean? It's noodles. It's a new place. So I was hoping to hear what he thought of the place. Did he like the way you have to approach the entrance through an alley? The whole place full of steam and noise. I was interested in how the vibe would seem to him. But he was on edge from the second we sat down. He kept sighing.

'Where have all these people come from?' he asked me. 'Didn't you ever think about that? Where are they from suddenly?'

'What do you mean, Robin?'

'This place is packed,' he said. And when I told him I was just pleased to see it doing well, he scoffed at me. He curled his lip. At this point, I began thinking he might have been drinking alcohol before coming to meet me.

'I guess it's not your kind of place,' I said. 'That's OK.'

'I didn't say that,' he snapped. 'I'm just commenting.'

'OK, sorry.'

For a while we ate in silence, well, not silence, because he was rather a loud eater. I ordered some beers, which he drank twice as fast as I did. The beer loosened him up a bit, but then the conversation didn't get much of a chance to flow. Every time I wanted to talk about the tableware, for example, he'd change the subject. He continuously jumped from one subject to another, sometimes snarling over himself as he changed direction.

First he was talking about his role, how it had changed since the company he worked for became assimilated into the Capmeadow project.

'What am I even doing at this stage? I literally have no idea what I'm meant to be focused on,' he said.

'It's a discovery phase,' I said. I was trying to be reassuring. 'We all have time to improvise to a certain extent, and find new ways to help each other and the company.'

This did not satisfy him. Then he moved on to the situation at Capmeadow more generally. He kept looking out of the window, and at his watch. He kept playing with his collar.

It felt like we were in the noodle bar for about an hour before I said, 'Robin, are you nervous because we're doing this as a date? Because I think you need to relax a bit. There's no pressure.'

I patted him on his hand, which had tensed almost into a fist on the table. His hand relaxed as I touched him, but his face became still and grave, which was not what I had hoped would happen.

'It's got nothing to do with being on a date,' he said. 'It's you. You just make me nervous.'

I felt my stomach turn cold when he said this. His face was grave. I could tell that he was ready to go on and unburden himself of something, apparently something awful about me.

'What? How can I make you nervous?'

'I never know what I can say in front of you.' This he almost whispered.

'What does that mean?' I asked.

'You know what I mean!' he said. He was whispering but also shouting. 'It's not your fault but, please don't pretend not to know what I mean.'

I didn't say anything. A lot of people have issues trusting me because of my job recording the feelings of colleagues about life at Capmeadow. I assumed he meant that, and I dealt with the issue by moving to the next solid and helpful thing I could think of.

'You can say whatever you want to me,' I said. 'We're not at work now.'

'But we are! We're always at work!'

He started laughing at this point, and the waiter arrived with another tray of drinks.

'Hey,' Robin said suddenly, startling the waiter. 'Hey man, where do you live?'

'I'm sorry, sir? I'm not sure I know what you mean . . .'

'You understand the question? I'm asking, where do you live? Do you live here at Capmeadow? What's your deal? Do you commute in?'

There was a moment of silence that felt like it would go on forever. Robin's eyes were glassy. He looked, I have to say, really like a predatory animal. A dog I once saw on a film had eyes like that, and that dog was starving hungry.

'I'm sorry,' I said to the waiter.

'It's OK,' the waiter said, and he left us as quickly as he could.

I had to explain to Robin that obviously this question was not something you can ask a stranger. It's highly sensitive personal data. Robin shook his head. He laughed – but not with any humour. There was a darkness in his face that I really didn't like at all.

'You can't talk to people like that,' I said again. 'It's fine to be curious, but some people don't like it.'

'What about you then?' he said.

'What about me?'

'Tell me something about you – tell me about your parents.'

For a long time, I didn't know what to say. And then I must have said something because I remember him looking at me, and his face went through a series of strange changes. At first he seemed sad, and then he seemed absolutely terrified, and then he went back to normal. I don't recall what I said to him. I believe I told him the story about going camping, the one with the cicadas. It's funny because I don't remember much of that story. I know we went away, and I remember all the hedges very high up on either side of the car at one point, and we drove for hours and hours, and I began to wonder if we were going underground because the hedges rose up so high on either side of the narrow road, like a tunnel of green light. I could hear my parents talking. I've lost their sound though, now. My parents' voices, their movements, they are gone from me. I— anyway.

We didn't mention it again. The truth is, I had a normal childhood. I don't have a very good memory because of something that happened when I was about eight years old. I don't remember much after that time, but I had a normal childhood. I went to school. My parents loved me, sometimes they were sad. Sometimes they were happy. It was normal. At the age of around eight, I lost them. It seems like I have blocked out a lot of what happened after that. It's funny isn't it? I must have been cared for. I must have been loved – I know that absolutely, someone loved me. Someone was there, always, and I never felt like I was in danger. I must have been sad and confused and hungry and all of those other things I am now. But I don't – ah. I feel like I should stick to the story about my date with Robin.

After I had told him – I guess – something about my early life and my experience here at Capmeadow, there was a kind of silence. I felt hurt, somehow. Really like I hadn't deserved this feeling. He really was spoiling the whole thing, and I was considering how to get out of there. Robin was looking at me now with an unguarded dislike. Neither professional nor date-appropriate.

He seemed to want to say something but he couldn't find the right words He made a strange slurring noise. I was by now completely unhappy and wanted to go home. I attended a quick one-to-one side-meeting which was requested urgently, while Robin scratched at something on his arm. The one-to-one meeting finished after a minute or so, and then I explained to Robin that the date was over.

He nodded. He seemed very unhappy and eager to be on his way. There was something defeated about the way he got his coat and offered to help me on with mine.

'I had a nice time, anyway,' I said.

'Did you?'

'I did. Before things became difficult, I was having a nice time. And anyway, it was good to be out with someone.'

'Out!'

'Yes, out. We went out together.'

He sighed. 'Whatever you say,' he said.

When we emerged from the noodle bar, I noticed a subtle change in the volume of the space around us. We walked to the end of the alley, through the steam and past the complicated walls of ducts and pipes that seemed to burst out and return into the building like worms. Tentacles, I thought to myself again.

When we got back to the street, my suspicions were confirmed – there had been a short expansion phase while we were eating dinner – there was now more street than there had been before. All around us, there was a general commotion. A couple walking past hurriedly seemed to be complaining about not being given any notice. They hunched like it was raining, though the dark sky was cloudless.

I saw Terri from the estates team running down the street. There was a sort of electricity in the air, which I find happens when some really significant progress has been made. A greasy sort of feeling, that whitens the eyes, you know, cleans out the throat.

'Terri!' I said. 'How nice to see you. What's going on? Is everything all right?'

'Sort of. There's been another expansion phase.'

'Oh really?' I said. 'That *is* sudden! I didn't hear about it, but then I don't get every email.'

Despite having to sound sort of concerned and professional, I actually felt completely alive again, and the drabness of my date with Robin was forgotten. I felt taller, like excess energy from the hard changes of expansion had somehow touched me.

Terri looked very tired. Her coat was drenched. Her hair was frayed and covered in grey droplets. She had been running for some time, it seemed. But it was a good tired. I wanted to touch her.

'What have they built this time?' I asked. 'Or is it just groundwork?'

There was a moment in which Terri looked at me and slightly shook her head, as though even she couldn't believe how big all of this was.

'There's a museum,' she said when she'd caught her breath. Her face was shuddering a little. 'A fucking museum.'

'Oh wow! A museum?'

'There's not supposed to be a museum,' Terri said.

'Oh right,' I said. 'But wow. It's there anyway! What kind of museum?'

'The Capmeadow Museum of Life, apparently,' she said. 'There's a sign.'

The Capmeadow Museum of Life! I mean, I had to control myself a little bit, but I felt very connected and thrilled by this idea. A museum. Honestly, even now, it feels like the greatest concept you could have come up with. I needed to get there. To see it.

'Terri,' I said. Actually gripping her arm now. 'I know you must be exhausted, but I'm sorry, it sounds amazing. A museum! Just amazing. Can you take me to see it?'

But even as I said it, I realised that Robin was with me, and he would not like to hear about this museum. To him, somehow, this sudden existence of a museum would definitely be a bad thing. And I did think, for a plunging flickering second, in that moment that Robin might be right. I always do that, I always default to thinking that someone else must be right, and I must be wrong. Even something as substantial as a completely new museum that represents us as a community in this expanding workplace.

Robin blurred a little bit in my peripheral vision, which is normally a sign that I am overthinking things.*

Anyway, I am who I am, so I repeated, 'Terri, I really want to see this museum. I think I need to go there, in fact.'

Terri smiled at me, but she was still not sure. 'Ugh, I don't really want to go back there, but OK, sure, I guess.'

I turned to Robin. 'Hey Robin, do you want to go and see the museum?'

As expected, Robin was being sullen. 'I thought you said the date was over,' he said.

'That date is over. But if you want, we can try another date, this time at the museum!'

'With her as well?'

He gestured at Terri.

'Yes, with Terri. She discovered the museum. You don't mind, Terri? It's really not a proper date. Robin and I are not remotely compatible. I think he should join us though – if he wants to. I think at least this will give us both a memorable experience.'

Terri looked unsure. She and Robin kept looking at each other. People do this with me sometimes – they look at each other and do things with their faces, communicate things they

---

* **Archivist's note:** It is fascinating, this blurring, when you see what actually happens in the footage. The effect is more like a flickering. I am recording this here because I always seem to forget the looks on the faces of the people who flicker, but in this moment, Robin, in the footage, which is grainy in the extreme, Robin is struggling to exist. There's no other way to describe it. He looks like he is being strangled. His eyes are bulging one second and then the next they are – or seem to be – smaller than peas. There is too, if you go frame by frame, extreme rage. Just burning pain and anger. At least, that's how it looks, but it's probably just my imagination. Don't forget, I have been alone for a long time, and at some point I will need a second pair of eyes on all this. Unless I have deleted it all, which I probably will.

think I don't notice. I am used to it. I'm so used to it, I feel like it's part of who I am to experience this stuff.

Since I was in school, or what I can remember of school, things always felt like they were fine if it was just me and one other person, but as soon as there was a group, people would communicate too quickly, or they would curve their communication around me. Like refracted light, it would bend around me. And I was in the dark. But my parents, my father, understood. He said to me, you can either try and be like everyone else, or you can be yourself and do what you want to do and let everyone else come along with you. It wasn't very snappy, but I think it's better that he was not always succinct because this was more accurate. I do wish I could remember his voice, his real sound.

'It's a long walk,' Terri said, glancing back in the direction she had been running from.

'That's OK! I really think I would walk all night for a sudden museum, Terri!'

'I feel sure it was terrifying!' she said. She didn't sound sure. This was her trying to dissuade me, I think. After a long silence, she agreed to take us back to the museum.

Robin came with us, which was a shock, though he continued to be sullen as we walked through freshly laid streets, still spongy underfoot where the material had not yet hardened.

It was quite a long walk, and as we went I saw several new beginnings, cleared areas lined with new-style accommodation buildings, shapes coming into focus as individual chalets and convenience shops. A place selling skiwear – or seeming to be a place selling skiwear – caught my eye and I made a note to bring myself back down here as soon as I could.

This new area was not a shock to me – the Capmeadow expansion had entered the more accelerated phase. Robin looked even more annoyed as we moved through the new streets. 'I'm at home,' he said. 'I'm cooking dinner.'

People say this kind of thing to me sometimes, but I really don't pay much attention. I've been told it doesn't matter – I am inclined to say it must matter somehow, but of course, not in the moment. It will be collected as feedback, and we will iterate on the current situation, I feel sure. At night, especially, I feel sure that this will be the case. But people say it to me, and in the moment, I have to actively move past their words.

'I'm on the stairs,' that's another one. People don't seem to notice they're doing it. I asked about it when it first happened; on that occasion, I asked someone who had come to see me why they just said, 'I'm looking in the wardrobe for a glove that I have lost,' and they had no recollection of saying it.

I was informed via email that it was something everyone did from time to time, and that it was natural. I asked if I was doing it, and I was given every reassurance that anything I was doing or not doing was completely normal too.

'There's a fog space coming up,' Terri said.

Robin sighed again and put on his face covering. I don't mind the fog so I didn't bother. My suit, which I had just recently bought from the small mall, is completely frictionless. None of the vapour makes it dirty. (By the way, the new mall, have you been? Because I have many recommendations if you would like them on where to get coffee and where to get the most amazing katsu sandos.)

As we stepped into the fog, I felt Robin pull away from the group.

'I am meant to be somewhere else,' he kept saying. 'I am on the landing. I can hear my mother and father talking about dinner. I am visiting my parents, what the fuck is happening? They're old, they need my help to lift things.'

These outbursts no longer bother me, but since I am here to be honest, I will say that I was hurt by his angry tone. I felt guilty somehow, which is something I struggle with, which is partly why I have come here to speak today.

The truth is, I feel this guilt, on some level, all the time. I don't let anyone see it, but the guilt is there, something I have done wrong, or must have done wrong, but I can't recall what it is. It must be nothing, really, that's what I would tell someone if they came to me with a vague feeling of guilt. I would say, 'While I am not a professional in this regard, by any means, I think it's very likely that if you don't remember doing something wrong, then you almost definitely didn't do anything wrong. That nagging feeling that you are guilty can come from other people, it can come from a sense that they have about themselves and they spread it around, they put it onto you.' That's what I would say to someone with these feelings. And also, thank you for sharing, I would always make sure to say thank you for sharing.

In the mist I tried to find Robin; I reached out for him, but he was no longer there.

'We've lost Robin,' I said.

'He's gone back,' Terri said. 'He's not here now.' She didn't look round. 'Follow me please, it's bad this fog. Worse than I've seen in a while.'

Terri wore a guiding light on her rucksack, which I kept a close eye on.

Very faintly, I thought I heard her say, 'I am in a taxi, on my way to visit my nephew.'

I should have worn a mask after all. After a few minutes, I felt the impurities in the mist clinging to my skin and I made the mistake of rubbing my eyes. I stumbled and the world shifted, vision completely left me, I could only see milk. I fell onto one knee. Terri's floating backpack light seemed to be a long way off.

I tried to call out, but my throat caught some of that impure mist, and I began coughing. It was ridiculous. I've been in and out of that mist as part of my job for as long as I can remember, and I never get bothered by it. But now I was panicking. Crawling around on the unfinished surface, which makes that particular noise.

I had the feeling I could see other people in the mist, small, like children. They didn't seem real, and could easily have been the beginnings of new bollards. There are no children in Capmeadow, I remember thinking that. But I felt sure that once there had been many of them. A room full of children, I remember.*

Beneath me, as I staggered, still coughing, towards where I thought Terri had gone, I felt the surface harden. It did not feel like the normal newly completed underfoot surface. I think it was actually unworked land. Not bedrock, but something else. Turning to my left, I saw lights moving away, twin red lights, a vehicle. But this couldn't be possible because vehicles of this kind are not permitted on the business park.

I felt a hand on my sleeve and was being pulled up and forward. I started coughing again, and trying to apologise for coughing onto the person pulling me along. After a few blind steps, I finally felt the fog curl away. Terri was standing in front of me, dripping wet. Behind her there were groups of colleagues,

---

* **Archivist's note:** There is no record of this, and yet, I feel sure she is correct. I look for evidence of children in Capmeadow all the time. Everything tells me it has happened. I have again, just now, spent hours looking, and found nothing. But the archive seems endless. Somewhere there must surely be the children of Capmeadow. (This is my own name for them.)

conducting meetings, conversing, and yet also, from time to time, breaking away to stare in awe up at the new development space. There was a strange hush over what was, I now saw, a vast piazza.

'It's worrying people,' Terri said. 'People are very concerned, I think.'

But I didn't really catch what she said next. Terri was no longer audible to me, because behind her, on the far side of the luxurious square, was the museum. The Capmeadow Museum of Life.

Transcribed footage #1:
Tom Crowley searches

The streets of Capmeadow, chewed at the edges, night here in the outer limits. The video footage is fresh and snappy. The foundation surface area (the ground they walk on) is juicy, and has not yet fully set. In the corner of the picture a dog has strayed into the zone and tugs heavily at the material, chewing it like leather. Something startles the animal and it flees. A shape pursues it. There is no sound. Slowly, the chewed-on ground heals and grows over itself. The slightly damp edges harden and form into paving. In the far distance, a mound rises, preparing to become a building of some kind. It looks large. It could be a new clothing outlet store, or a waffle house – the size suggests something fairly grand. A mist draws in.

Tom Crowley discusses innovative work–life balance and Oliver Cromwell

My mother's house was the same as it had always been, though it was a different building to the one I grew up in. She moved from house to house, depending on landlords, depending on circumstance. After ten years of being retired, she was more exhausted than ever, freelancing for former employers. The stress that she wasn't doing enough to justify the invoices she tentatively submitted each month was palpable. She was also understandably bored to death with the housework. A layer of grease lay under the layer of dust on all the piled-up recipe books in the kitchen. I was given the spare room.

'You can have some space in the wardrobe, but don't spread out too much.'

'I won't,' I said. 'I wouldn't.'

'Some of that stuff is the lodger's. The old lodger I mean. He will be back for it.'

I looked at the sad collection of nothingness, two matching baby blue shirts folded badly on top of each other. A creased leather laptop bag, a small stack of *GQ* magazines, funeral shoes, all carefully stowed into the partitioned areas of the wardrobe.

'I've put the coffee on,' she said and then left me.

I waited a few minutes in the silent room, and then I went to stand with her in the kitchen. There was no space for me to lean or sit, so we just stood. There had been a dog for a while, but now it was just her again. The kettle was too loud, she was saying. It was meant to be silent, and had been very good when she first got it from the little cheap homeware shop in town.

'Things never get beyond a good start,' she said. 'Something always has to happen.'

I nodded. She handed me a coffee and looked at me. I felt like I was being peered at through a hole in a cell door.

'I won't be here long,' I said.

'What about work? Do they know you're here?'

'Well, yeah, I mean, not the exact address, but yeah, they know the doctor said I should get away for a while.'

She made a noise and her lips tightened.

'What?'

'Nothing! I'm just surprised your doctor said that. I'd have thought you needed to keep things normal. To be with your family as much as possible – that's what I would want.'

'It's not that simple,' I said. 'I'm to stay away so I can relax and let the whole thing become a memory, but like the memory of a dream.'

'The memory of a dream?' She looked at me sideways.

'It's complicated. But yes, basically. I won't be here long.'

'It doesn't sound like it *needs* to be complicated, though, does it? It sounds pretty simple to me: you had a funny turn. People have been having these things for years. Your uncle Lance used to go Australian.'

'What do you mean he would go Australian? Lance wasn't Australian.'

'That's what I'm saying! Whole weeks, he'd talk with an Australian accent, and you couldn't stop him.'

'This isn't the same,' I said. 'Uncle Lance was putting it on. He probably thought it was another good way to give Aunt Maureen The Willies.'

'Well, either way, if you ask me, you should be back home with them. I'm not trying to tell you what to do. I don't know what you've been through. But I'm surprised. It's surprising that a doctor would tell you to leave them all in the lurch.'

'It's the advice I was given, that's all,' I said. 'Not even advice, you know, like, this is what you have to do. Doctor's orders.'

We sat in silence and she drained her coffee. 'Doctor's orders,' she muttered.

I looked around at the quietness of her home. It was in mourning, really, for the dog. I had loved the dog, I found myself crying that she was no longer alive. My coffee went cold.

'Why don't you have a bath?' I heard my mother say. She was outside.

'Yeah, maybe.'

I went upstairs intending to get ready for a bath, but instead I spent the next few hours lying on the bed in the spare room, looking at the uneven bookshelf I had assembled from a flatpack at the age of fourteen. It was still lined with most of the books I was reading at that time, and the few years that followed. They were often gifts, the books I had accumulated. I tried to picture the various people who had given them to me. There were several I had never read. Two were handbooks for the expanded Capmeadow project. Some were just old Irvine Welsh paperbacks.

'Hey, Mum, when did these handbooks arrive?'

'What?'

'In here – when did these Capmeadow books arrive?'

'I'm going out,' she said. I heard the door close downstairs. I considered taking one of the handbooks out. It was very thick, and one of them was faded like the books around it, where it had been in direct sunlight for a long period of time. I found I couldn't face lifting the handbook. I lay back and looked at the ceiling.

As I lay there, I could smell the mist at Capmeadow rolling in again. It fell upon me like a weighted blanket. I drifted.

Someone sent me an email during this time; I could barely move, but I read the email carefully. I was being offered a new contract, with new terms and a range of new benefits. I accepted the terms from my position on the bed, paralysed by the smell of the mist.

Later, I ran a bath.

'Not all the hot water please!' She was back.

'I know, Mum.'

I sat on the edge of the bath, facing the mirror. My body felt and looked weak. My shoulders were bony. My chest and stomach had lost tone, my skin seemed to sag from the forehead down. I looked away from the mirror. I should take advantage of this time, I thought, get fit, improve my physique. Improve my mental health. I imagined myself running around the park in the town where I grew up. How many failed cross-country attempts had I had on the slopes of the park? Being the absolute slowest in the entire year. I was trying to go too fast, was the problem. I know now to run slowly, to keep off the lung burn. I knew also that I would not go running at all. Maybe a walk. Maybe some press-ups.

I let the sound of the water just roar for a while. I listened in on a fireside chat with the head of research and analytics. The water was so loud, I felt myself almost airborne within it, and yet the voice of the head of research and analytics was clear as a bell. You could hear her many years of experience as a behavioural scientist, her obvious joy at being able to put her PhD to good use, and yet the roaring of the water seemed to have separated me from my body. I was airborne, that's how it felt. Not flying, but in the air, no part of myself seemed to be touching anything. The art of good data, the head of research and analytics was saying, is to ask good questions. Spend longer than you think you need to writing the questions. Spend twice as much time on this than you think you need to. All the metrics in the world can't save you if you have asked people a load of dumb old shit. I was completely inside the sound of running water, and also I felt like the head of research and analytics had confirmed a technique I myself had always used, which was to think probably longer than most people would consider productive about what research questions I would want to ask. My lateness with all my work felt validated. Also my body was numb.

'I need a bath too later! Please don't use it all!'

I stopped the tap and lowered my body into the bath, sinking straight through the mean layer of foam I had managed to get going with the bodywash. The plug in my mother's bath had been bought by a handyman on behalf of the landlord. It fit the plughole so badly, I had to wad it with toilet roll. Already by the time I'd sorted it out, the water in the bath had gone down from a normal depth to barely covering my thighs. I shivered in there for I don't know how long. My mother's bathroom gurgled around me, the sound of the heating came and went. At one point, there was a twenty- or thirty-second power cut, which was almost nostalgic. These short losses of service were something that seemed to follow my mother around from rented house to rented house. Poor heating, bad wiring, some furniture that could not be removed but that was clearly not the right size for the rooms. She's made it work her whole life, lived in the gaps other people created with no thought at all, a chucked-together life. She amazes me.

When the lights came back on, I heard her talking down-stairs, a video call, I could hear the sound of my children in the background, the pitch breaking as they scraped their chairs in the kitchen and screamed at the cat.

Later, around 5 p.m., I had a call from HR. Just a check-in, the HR specialist said. There will be some changes to your work-ing arrangements when you return, they told me. I remember I was looking at my feet on the green carpet of the stairs in my mother's house while I received that call. White socks that had grown shapeless around the toes, crushing into the pile of the carpet, and then they were on the carpet of the office, the tight, hard-wearing surface of the corridor. I am on my way to see you, I said into the phone to the HR specialist.

'It's normal for you to feel that way,' came the reply. 'Don't think about it too much.' The HR specialist asked me about my mood. I said it was not the best.

'It's normal for you to feel that way too,' they said.

'I really feel like I'm in the office and I'm on my way to see you,' I said.

'No, that's not happening.'

The call ended and my mother said I should go to bed for a while. It was about 6 p.m. I slept until the morning. When I woke up, it was raining heavily. The white bones of my mother's birch rocked confidently in the garden. There had been an aunty of my father's, I think, who had suffered from birch disease when she was in her mid-sixties. Birch disease is where your bones start to diverge and sprout like roots. They send new bone growth into the major blood and nerve systems of your body. It is a fatal and irreversible condition, my father told me.

By the time a person with birch disease dies, they have a bone structure that looks like a silver birch tree in autumn. Frail networks bounce and flex inside the coffin, as everything else is eaten away. If a person with birch disease has a fall, my father told me, they do not crash like a normal person, but spring back up in places, like a fallen branch does if you drag it along the street.

When the skin around the bones is broken, the bones split out catastrophically, in a kind of explosion captured and frozen in time. The patient looks like a tree in winter. This is called *flourishing*, that's what my father told me. Flourishing is disastrous for the sufferer of birch disease. The bones sway like wires, and the arteries and veins they were tracked to split and fall away. Sometimes a patient can flourish alone and be found there white as a birch, completely drained of blood.

I can remember where we were when he explained all of this to me. I was quite young, and we were spending Christmas with him at my grandmother's house. My mother was not well, and was staying with her sister in Leeds. I had gone outside to hide in the coal bunker. He came out to smoke a cigarette when he noticed me in the bunker. 'Well look at you,' he said. 'Covered in soot like Father Christmas.'

Then he told me that story about birch disease. I have no idea why he told me that story.

'You're too young to remember,' he said, 'the Christmas when your aunt died from flourishing.'

I can't recall the name of the aunt. I knew it wasn't true, of course – that the disease did not exist, or if there was such a disease, then it wouldn't really happen the way he was describing. This flourishing he had described was just to frighten me. Whenever I asked him about it later, he pretended not to understand what I was talking about.

Hey, have you completed that assignment? my father was asking me. He had phoned and asked to talk to me.

What assignment, Dad?

The training for fire safety in your office building, he said.

It was a video call. He was there asking me this now, his blood vessels like wires coming out of him. He had my face, but my face under incredible pressure and white to the point of greyness. You should really complete your return-to-work interviews as early as possible, he said.

I turned my phone off. My father died when I was only in my twenties. I considered removing all the work-based apps from my phone, but I didn't go through with it. As I was considering it, I just lay still. My father's appearance was not unexpected. In the same way that Hen's presence felt false, so too had his at times. When he'd break character and tell me some grizzly story. Or challenge me to a physical test I couldn't possibly complete – do 500 press-ups before dinner. Read an entire book before the morning. The next time I'd see him, he would be back to his normal self. Sober, daydreaming, closing his eyes in order to focus on what the radio was saying.

I wondered if I was becoming like him. Did he experience this same event with me? Did I appear to vanish and then crop up again, having never been anywhere? Maybe that was why he said all that rotten shit to me.

I thought about him for a while. I considered whether, despite the doctor's relaxed attitude about the whole thing, some handed-down cerebral fissure had silently detonated inside me on that commute, and now I was the one. I was the one about to say twisted things to them. I was the one invading the private moments of my children and making their experience of their home life strange and frightening. It was right that I had come away. I was doing it for them. I was protecting them.

The rain fell on my mother in the garden. Through the spare-room window, I saw pick her way along the little path towards the sheltered area with a newspaper over her head and a large yellow mug of coffee in her hand. She looked exhausted and small. She sat down in the sheltered area on one of her cast-iron seats. Furnitures, she called them. Whenever she got garden chairs and tables, she referred to them as furnitures, in the plural. I never knew why. There would've been a story explaining this. Perhaps my brother or sister had called them that, or my stepfather when he was still alive. I wasn't privy to the reason, I just had to go along with it.

She saw me looking down at her and waved the paper through the air over her head; she smiled, but immediately after I had waved back, she looked away from me, opened the paper and fetched a pen from her garden jacket. She began attacking the crossword. I felt keenly what a heavy weight I must be to have in this little house with her. I went to the bathroom and washed myself, without going to the trouble of a full bath this time.

I went out into town. I bought a packet of tissues. I heard people in the newsagent's talking, while I pretended to look at the soup. It was the same boy – though now a man clearly in his late thirties – the same boy who had always worked here. He was the manager now. He was talking to someone else who I recognised, but who would not have known me at all. They were speaking in mutters. Our town has an accent made entirely of mutters and unspoken consonants.

'She looks sick, you know? I saw her in the Cottage. She's stopped eating.'

I didn't like the tone of their voices. This person sounded vulnerable, whoever they were talking about, and yet, always in that muttering dialect, there is a cruel kind of mirth. A happiness that someone is not eating, is wandering in and out of places.

'Total chaos wherever that one goes. Who's looking after her, eh?'

They made noises and grunts about who would look after whoever this was. Their meaning was hard to glean.

'Anyway, she's not legal to drink, but she tried anyway. Asking everyone to buy her a drink. Embarrassment, mate.'

A car horn burped outside and the customer gossiping swore. 'Fucksake. I only left him in the car five minutes. Stupid bloody kids.'

I heard him leave and came out from behind the soups. I nodded at the original corner-shop boy.

'All right?' I said. He nodded back, like always, recognition but no friendliness.

I moved more around the shop. I looked at the local headlines for missing-person stories, wondering if this gossip of theirs would be in there. And then, of course, for headlines and pictures of my daughter.

I was aware that this impulse was slightly insane of course, it was not logical. Hen was at home. I should really have been there with her. It was clearly unhealthy to be doing this in the newsagent's in my hometown, but I looked. I looked at the faces of kids going by, expecting one of them to be her.

They couldn't tell what I was doing, of course, but each time it happened, I felt a little bit more detached from things. More like a person on the fringes of society. Your daughter is at home, I reminded myself. She is safe and well. You've had an episode. You should not have come back here to this town.

I went to the castle. It's actually a ruin of a castle, in fact. It was made into a ruin a long time ago – by Oliver Cromwell. There is a sort of anger directed against Cromwell for that reason in the town where I grew up. 'We could've had a really nice castle here, if it wasn't for that miserable bastard!' That's what we thought. 'We could've had something beautiful. That miserable old prick!' We've all said it. We say it like Oliver Cromwell is still around, like he's in the current government.

The castle in the town where I grew up was made of the local stone, a red sandstone. You can rub it away with your thumb. Don't go to the castle, I said to myself. You need to get back to the city and to your life. Still not technically at the castle, but in its shadow, I rubbed at the stones of a lump of ruined wall. This was a good six hundred metres outside the main keep. This would've been a place of work, the castle, the little houses and shelters around it. All of these lumps of stone were once important to the industries of the time. I rubbed and powder came away in my hands. Beneath my feet was the carpet in the corridor that led from my office floor to the lifts and then down to the HR offices.

The mist that came into the space where a moat had been smelled the same as Capmeadow mist, that fragrance of heating ducts and food, of fields too, of soil, gravel smells, wet parkland, a density of landscapes crammed into a vapour. I entered a meeting.

'Sorry,' someone said, 'sorry to interrupt you, Catherine, but I think someone needs to go on mute.'

'Yeah, what is that sound? It's like a scraping sound?'

'Oh,' I said. 'Oh, sorry, I think that's me, I was just rubbing this bit of castle wall.'

'Are you even meant to be on this call, Tom?'

I didn't know how to answer. I ended my participation in the call and went back home to my mother's. All the time I walked, I looked for the face of my daughter in the streets, and worried that I was being alienated from my job. I have such a specific role, I was sure it would be impossible to find a job like it again. Definitely not at the same salary level. I wondered about the new contract I had signed. Did it weaken my position there? I realised I had barely read it. I hadn't even told Eliane about the new contract. What had it meant?

I was also sure that by now I was on some sort of list shared by HR people in companies of a certain size and valuation – this guy comes with a huge amount of baggage, it would probably say. Or he is totally lulu. I had to hold on to my place in the Capmeadow world. I thought all this as I passed the pubs and houses, houses and pubs that form the character of the place where I grew up, and also as I walked along the corridor that led from my floor to the floor on which the departments for engineering and product management were located.

At an agreed time, I spoke to Hen and her brother on a video call. 'They'll have been wondering what's going on,' my mother said, nodding at the screen. I could see Eliane, just out of shot.

'How's it going, El?' I asked.

'This is for them,' she said.

'Sure, we'll talk later then.'

She didn't say anything else. I saw the outline of her move completely off screen. The next time I heard her voice it was to give instructions to the kids.

'Tell Daddy what you've been doing at school. He's desperate to know I expect.'

I asked Hen, 'Have you had a good time? Do you understand why I'm not there?'

She shrugged and smiled. She seemed to be completely oblivious to the fact I had been away from home for a few days. Her face was pixelated, it swam and multiplied as she flung herself around and gurned at me.

'We're making Viking ships,' she told me.

'That'll be nice,' I said. 'Longboats. Are you building one?'

'We all have to.'

'Can I see it?'

'No, it's at school.'

I looked at the space around the screen, a way of resting my eyes from trying see her clearly. The rest of the words I was supposed to be saying faded away. My daughter flickered on the screen. She moved and chewed the air. I found myself close to tears.

'How about you, son?' I asked, trying to see him too.

'Yeah, fine,' my son said.

'All OK at school?'

'Yeah.' He smiled at me. I could see his entire face, his elongated chin, his purple-coloured braces. He was like a photograph of a clean, familiar landscape. In the background, his sister clattered and shifted.

'I need to talk to you both,' I said, with all the authority I could gather. 'I will be away here for a while longer, I'm afraid.'

My son said, 'We know. You're looking after Grandma.'

'That's right, I'm looking after Grandma.'

I tried to talk about it more, but I could hear Hen's voice, 'We know we know,' she said. 'It's fine Daddy don't worry.' And before long she was showing me trinkets from her bedroom, or things she had found. Always just not quite fitting her face into the screen. Never quite there. She took her brother's phone and held it up so I could see the latest photos he had taken of the cat.

Soon, they were gone. I felt exhausted.

'You can't stay here indefinitely,' my mother said. She was looking at me now from the shadows beyond the light of the computer screen.

'We'll both go round the twist,' she said.

I spoke to the office again that evening. More questions about the latest work I had submitted.

'The illustrators don't know what to do with your descriptions,' I was told. 'You're wasting a lot of people's time with these.'

The illustrators were meant to have created two sets of draw-ings, one, a motif of people gathering sensibly in an emergency congregation area, demonstrating the correct emergency pro-tocol. The other was meant to be a series of scenes depicting people cowering under their desks or ransacking the stationery rooms, fighting over resources. That sort of thing. I had been specific in the descriptions, but I couldn't recall the work now. It felt like many months had passed since I completed this brief.

'I don't understand this,' I said to Cath.

'Neither do I, Tom.' She sounded exhausted.

The images showed people in swamps. People just represented as eyes. In one image, the sense of complete isolation was so powerful, I had to look away.

'None of this is right,' I said. 'I didn't specify any of this.'

'Look, I think I need you here for this. Can you come in?'

I paused before answering. I could hear my mother muttering somewhere that the boiler was about to explode. She was asking, why does this always happen to me?

Something behind Cath Corbett caught my eye.

'What's going on with the kitchen, Cath?' I asked. 'It looks different. Have I been away for that long?'

Cath Corbett looked behind her towards the kitchen area.

'Oh, right, so we've moved the team to a new part of Cap-meadow. You'll see when you come in.'

Later that night I was there, on the Capmeadow estate. I don't remember the journey, but I was in the tropical gardens. The uplighting made me feel safe against the pitch dark. Far in the distance, I saw lights that could not have been there before, and great towers that seemed to be rising up. I thought of Hen lost out there among the cranes. Somewhere I heard a dog howling. And then, closer by, behind the elephant fern, I felt sure I saw an elbow. A dirty eye seemed to glare at me, from deep within the tropical garden foliage. It blinked, I am sure it blinked; there was breathing, this too I was certain of, a breathing that was shallow and frightened and lost. It was her!

I lunged into the leaves, I felt spikes and stiff branches cut into my face. Something – a branch? – caught the corner of my eye, scratching me quite badly. I felt the rip of my shirt. I pushed into a space that seemed to have had a shape plugged out, like someone had recently been there. Again the foliage shifted, and I slipped and fell forward, smacking my hands and my cheek into the coarse bark of a tree. I was stuck now, my feet were tangled in something down below me, it was too dark to see what it was, vines of some kind. If I moved my hands, I would fall further, and there were branches pushing into my nose, my eyes, tearing the skin on my neck. I wondered if I would die. I was looking directly into the centre of a twisted wooden eye. Somewhere I heard the sound of foxes. I called for help.

With difficulty, I managed a final push forward, hoping to free my ankles, but I didn't get far. I plunged deeper into the tropical foliage. I was soon lying down in the plants. The darkness closed in. I saw UX patterns, kanban boards with content placeholders, Jira tickets for work, and realised I was in another meeting. My hands reached out and touched slime. The base of the planting seemed layered in decomposing leaves.

'Can someone please turn off their microphone?'

'Yes, thank you, it's quite loud.'

'I can't mute them because it's not my meeting.'

The call cut out. I twisted myself and managed to lie on my back. I thought that somewhere I could hear voices. Only those monster-sized towers and lights were visible. The voices got louder. A security guard eventually found me.

'This has to stop, Tom,' he said. I let him help me up.

BEN PESTER

'Thank you,' I said as he brushed me down roughly. It was Steve, from the front desk.

'You can't come into the cloud garden,' he said. 'The humidity here is finely balanced. You can't come in here again.'

'I'm supposed to be in a meeting,' I said.

'The meeting has ended.'

Steve drove me to the station in silence. I declined three calendar invites on my way home, and by the time I arrived at my mother's, felt completely drained.

The next day, I took my mother out for a glass of rosé and a pub dinner. She wanted to talk to me about my health, she said. The implication was clear – she wanted me gone.

'I should go back,' I said to her. 'I know I should get back.'

'You've had such a shock,' she said, radiating relief that I was going to move back out of her home. I was not sure how many days it had been. 'You poor thing,' she said. She was tender now that I was definitely leaving. She felt guilty, I could tell. I didn't blame her for wanting her space, her life, back.

'I'm sorry it wasn't easy here,' she said. 'I'm used to being by myself now I suppose. I've got my own things to be getting on with.'

We were standing at the bar. She reached up to my face where I had scratched myself in the cloud gardens at Capmeadow. I was not ready for how old her hands felt.

'I'm not sure what to do, Mum,' I said. 'What if I can't cope?'

I felt a sudden rush of panic that has always come with confessing things to my mother. A splurging feeling that if I completely fall to pieces, she will have to pick me up, and what if she found that she could no longer manage it? What if we had passed that marker in our life, where even if she tried her

130

hardest, it would not be enough, if I really fell, she would not be able to stop me falling?

'Jesus, of course you will cope!' she said, slapping me on the arm. 'Honestly, nothing happened, Thomas. You need to get over that stupid day. It's only a day for god's sake! You had a funny turn.'

I agreed with her and we went to her favourite table to order and eat and drink our dinner. Later that evening, I left her at home and went out once again into the damp school-hall air of my hometown.

I went to the corner shop, nodded at the original corner-shop boy. I don't know why this was always a destination for me – the off-licence/post office near my mother's house. Well, I do know, it was an old temptation of mine. A tiny yearning to get back into the old life I had here. The two or three years in which I was only happy. I had no other feelings, or at least that's how it seems now. Or maybe, other than late homework, I had no guilt.

I struck out again to the old places, a repetition, but this time I went to search for a thread that would take me back to my childhood, some way of undoing all the mistakes I had made. To see if I could see my younger self and correct his errors. Or, more honestly, enjoy again his thrilling and foolish mistakes. I made my way into the town centre. Here, in this triangular stretch of pavement, I thought, how many hours have I waited for buses here, or said long farewells late at night? It smelled like the coffee bar in the A building at Capmeadow. I could hear the espresso machine, and I could hear the young barista chatting with the senior managers about his weekend. This was where, on a cold night, I kissed someone for the first time, and I cannot remember her name.

The sounds keep coming, the doors of Building A opening and closing, the passing by of colleagues who've just finished playing a game of squash at the nearby sports hall.

And younger, when I was younger, these places were not restaurants, but shops where my pocket money flashed away. And then this park was where we walked with my mother, after the violent first days of her separation from my father. Here in this street where we rented our first house without him, when all the doors seemed to be opening and closing all night, and kept my mother awake.

The weeping willow where my father lurked in the street watching our house one night. I saw him and thought he had come to see us, but in fact he was there to watch the man from the repossession company come and tow away the car he claimed was his own, and which my mother had been using to get to work, to take us to school. In the rain he crouched there, I saw his spectacled eyes as two white discs with the streetlight in them. Could he see me? Impossible not to. Impossible.

This park again which I've covered with my footsteps, every single slope of its hills, every trenched flooded bog, suddenly seemed to be leaking, it rose with the smell of the carpets in the corridor of Building B at Capmeadow, and I could hear people asking me how I've been. Alex Wood saying he thought I had quit, but he's really glad to see me. He seemed to really mean it. I touched the fading sandstone wall, and was in discussions with the illustrators, who seemed exasperated and precious about their expertise.

My phone buzzed heavily in my pocket when I was on the roof of the stone bunker overlooking the ruins of the castle.

'She's not well,' Eliane said. Her voice sounded exhausted, far away. 'Can you come back?'

I had already packed my bags, of course, but I found myself resisting. I need to stay longer, I was saying. I was saying that it was for the best, for all of us, if I stay away. 'I'm not well,' I said.

There was silence on the other end of the line. I wondered if this was the sound of my marriage ending. 'Are you still there?' I asked.

She laughed, just a single dry syllable.

'It's that bad?' I said.

'She thinks she's done something wrong. I'm not actually sure you being away is helping anyone. What are you doing now anyway?'

'I'm in the park.'

'That must be nice.'

There was a moment here where we would normally fight, but I felt the passion for it come and move away, like a bus.

'What's wrong with her anyway?' I asked. 'Her illness I mean. I hope it's not me. She doesn't know, does she? About this thing I'm going through, and which I will get sorted, I promise.'

'Why don't you talk to her, hang on.'

I couldn't think of anything to say to stop the phone being handed over to Hen. There was a whistling in the line.

'Hello?' I said.

A coldness came through the phone – a creaking, deep time cold. Then her voice. My daughter's voice.

'Daddy!'

'How are you, chicken? Mummy said you were feeling poorly.'

'Yeah.'

'What's the matter? Is it a stomach ache?'

The whistling noise returned. Hen's voice receding, fading in and out as though she was not holding the phone correctly.

'Hen, are you there?'

'Yeah. I'm sorry, Daddy.'

'What? Hey, Hen, why are you sorry?'

'I'm sorry for getting lost.'

I tried to get her to repeat what she had said, but the next voice was Eliane.

'She's gone. Sorry. She just goes like that.'

'It's OK,' I said. 'I miss you.'

'You know what to do then, Tom. Just come back. Let the kids see you. You've said it yourself a million times, whenever you're not feeling right, it's the kids who bring you back to yourself, so come home.'

I left my mother's house the next morning. I was back home just as the city was turning dark.

My son was waiting up in the little box room that had become the place where the kids would go to watch TV. The snug, we called it, but it was not snug in there. A back bedroom with two mismatched armchairs crammed next to each other. This is where the two of them spent most of their time. I had been gone for maybe a week, but he looked like he had aged years since I last saw him. I realised that I couldn't remember the last time I had spoken to my son. I was hanging by the door, in exactly the way he had done when he was smaller and would not want to go to bed and would think we didn't know he was there, breathing and sucking his fingers while we watched *Grand Designs*.

He stood up when he noticed me.

'You're up late,' I said.

'What? It's not even nine thirty,' he said, laughing.

His bedtime was nine, I was sure of it, but I must have been wrong. He wasn't arguing, but mocking me for not knowing. He stood up, and I could see that he was now taller than me.

'How've you been, sunshine?' I asked him. 'I've missed you.'

'Fine. Missed you too.'

The hug that came next engulfed me in a mass and a fragrance that was completely new. He was wearing perfume of some kind. He was muscular where he used to be reedy. It felt aggressive almost, his need to crush me in his arms, to let me know how strong he had become. But then I felt a kind of need in him. I had been away from him too long.

'Sorry I wasn't here this week,' I said.

'It's OK.'

'I'm back now though. It's good to see you.'

'It's good to see you, too,' he said.

We sat for a moment in the awkward room.

'You'll be getting ready for bed now then, please,' I said. He looked at me like I was crazy and curled his lip.

'Now please,' I said and stood up. He didn't stop what he was doing. I didn't want to fight, so I left him there without pushing it.

I stood on the landing. My daughter's room was in the loft above me – the naked stairs leading up there were still spattered with plaster and paint from the conversion. The *illegal* conversion, as an estate agent called it when we thought we might have to sell before it was finished. The light bulbs up there were also failing. The whole top half of the house flickered and buzzed. It was as though the house wanted us to know, to constantly know, of the chaos of trying to pay for all of this. Of trying to hold everything together. I felt exhausted. I could see the shape of my son still in the snug, the television flickering. His solid, enormous shadow.

He used to be so small; I'd hold him and he'd climb all over me, and it was nothing, he weighed nothing at all. Soft sweet bones, hair that dazzled me, huge eyes. My boy!

The door creaked as I moved nervously back into the room, the snug, with him. I sat myself on the chair where Hen normally sat. My son was watching an animated film, manga kind of thing, every few seconds someone would leap through the air screaming with rage. Someone else was confused and suddenly panicked.

'I love you, sunshine,' I said after a minute or so. It felt useless. I touched his hand. I hugged his neck by leaning over from my chair to his and hooking him towards me. I could detect somewhere an impending calendar entry. An appointment of some kind.

'Love you too, Dad.'

'How has it been here?'

There was a fight on the screen. Blood, spit, sweat, lines to denote extreme movement. I think he made a noise, but we were both transfixed by the violence. After a while someone's body was sliced in half from the right shoulder down through the left hip.

'I'm just going to go and get a glass of water,' I said. 'Do you want anything?'

'Some water please, Dad.'

'Sure. Back in a sec.'

On the way down the stairs, I emailed Cath Corbett to find out if we should have a catch-up of some kind. She replied instantly, asking me to switch to the messaging app. It was a new one I didn't recognise. The download took a while. I was still on the stairs. I sensed my son go past me, muttering something about getting his own water. I heard my daughter's bedroom door open and close upstairs. I glimpsed her legs on the landing as she went to use the toilet. Then I was chatting to Cath Corbett; we discussed an issue relating to microcopy on an onboarding form that was being shared internally to all employees.

A button currently said SUBMIT, but Cath Corbett wanted to change it to APPROVE. I advised that we should keep it as SUBMIT as that was what you did – you submitted the form. Someone called Ash Maltby wanted to just use DONE. More people joined the chat. I was still on the stairs. Someone said actually we needed to rethink the form itself – should it be a form or a series of modals? The action was, after all, meant to be outside the main use of the application. Cath Corbett whispered *shit* under her breath. I became aware that my daughter kept squeezing past me on the stairs, and had given me a small hug each time. I was still on the stairs, and I let people in the meeting know that I was just on the stairs. I was on the stairs as my wife went by, and I thought about telling everyone in the meeting how hard it was becoming to breathe. I cannot breathe, I wanted to say, I cannot breathe in the pale air of my marriage. But I held back, I didn't say this. As the meeting went on, I felt myself thinking less and less about the stairs. I began to sense more and more of myself to be in a comfortable seat at my desk, with lighting above that replicated the exact wave frequency of a sunset.

I could smell dinner being prepared. It felt like the wrong time for dinner. Also, it was supposed to be my job to make the dinner, especially on this day, the day of my return to the family after a few days away. I was still on the stairs a long time after everyone had eaten their dinner; the kids were in bed, the moonlight was coming down through the window in the now empty snug where my son had been earlier that day. I went to bed with a kind of vibration across my skin. Eliane didn't turn over when she woke up. I heard her sigh but she stayed where she was with her back to me. I said goodnight. After a while, she turned over and spoke to me.

'I'm tired,' she said.

'I know, get some sleep.'

'I can't continue like this.'

'I know. I'm sorry.'

She didn't reply. She sighed again. The pale air, the difficulty breathing, it all crept back in. I struggled to swallow. It felt urgent that I should reassure her. I was not treating her fairly at all.

'I promise,' I said. 'It's finished. I don't know what happened, but I am feeling better. I've been given new work, so at least the job is safe.'

She clutched the pillow angrily. 'Of course your job is safe! This is what I mean, Tom. I'm tired of living with this level of panic. The ground is never stable.'

She had said these things to me before, I realised, but it felt like this was the last time she would say them before she finally left me. I was convinced she wanted to leave me.

'It is stable. The ground is stable, I promise. I'm feeling much better. A bit of time out helped. You know,' I said, 'the time I spent with my mother has really helped. She isn't lonely, not really, but I couldn't live like that. I lie awake at night thinking about what would happen if I lost you. I'm so frightened of it,' I said. 'I'm just so scared of losing you that all the shape of me breaks down. I don't feel right until I see you again. And it's the same with the kids. It's worse with the kids. The idea of losing one of them – I can't cope with it.'

'You're not losing us!' Eliane sat up in the bed now. She rubbed her face and sighed again. I felt wretched knowing I was the one making her sigh like this.

'You're unhappy,' I said. 'It's my fault.'

'Jesus Christ! This is what I mean. You don't understand what it's like for us when you start spiralling.'

'I'm not spiralling.'

'When did you even last wash?'

'What kind of a question is that! I have been working, that's all. If it's bothering you, I can go and wash now. I can have a quick shower.'

'Don't be stupid. You'll wake the whole house. I'm just saying, you can't just tell me you're better when you obviously aren't.'

By this point, we were both wide awake. Eliane flopped back onto the pillow. I was still just lying there. I spoke into the space between the mattress and the pillow. From time to time I could feel her breath, already with the fragrance of sleep on it.

'I know you're doing your best,' she said. 'It's just that I can't tell how you're going to react to pressure. I feel like if I ask you to consider even the smallest thing outside of our routine, you will collapse under the weight of it. You need to stop catastrophising our lives.'

'Eliane, I'm not catastrophising. I had a completely real nightmare. It was *the* nightmare. She was gone. She was with me, I could still feel the warmth of her hand in my hand and . . .'

'Oh Jesus stop it. Just stop. It.'

But I couldn't stop it. We argued more and at some point in the night, I left the bed. I left the room. I left the house.

I don't remember how I got back to Capmeadow. They found me in the car park, the night security team. They asked me if I wanted to talk to someone. They brought me into a room I had never seen before. I was asked if I would like a place to sleep for a few hours, which I agreed to. When I woke up, I was in a kind of pod – like a rigid indoor tent. Instead of a zip, it had a small door at the foot of the bed. There was a hotel-style package on the bed with a fresh pair of pants, socks and a T-shirt.

When I emerged, I was in a large hall; it could have had any purpose, but at the moment it was filled with these igloo-like pods, dozens of them, all exactly like the one I had just emerged from. I found myself wondering how I had woken. There had been no alarm clock. I was in the office. I had emerged from a pod. There were colleagues around me. People I recognised, but not enough to nod at or say hello to.

A whole range of people, too. Obvious managers, graduate-track analysts, all just having a look around and smoothing over the questions about why they had started sleeping at the office, and what woke them up, and which part of the business complex they were currently in. There were windows, but high up, along the walls. It reminded me of the school sports hall. When I had been at secondary school, this was a place I often dreamt of sleeping in. We would try to find reasons for this to happen. A charity sleepover in the school, for example. We never did it, and I think I wanted it to happen more than my friends did. I tried to remember my friends from school. What would they think of me now? Nothing. I can't picture any of them thinking anything. We've come a long way, I thought to myself.

People were heading towards a sign at one end of the hall – the universal sign for showers. I followed along. I wondered how my family would be doing. Would Eliane still be asleep? I considered texting, but my phone was in my pod. It didn't matter, I told myself. The important thing was to find Hen. She must be frightened, I thought. Nothing else really mattered. It didn't even matter that of course Hen was at home. She must have been because I saw her – but what did I see? An arm, the flip of her heel. I was half asleep but I was more sure than ever – and I am sorry for going back to this, but my daughter was missing. And it had been many days now.

I wondered if she was here, if she was frightened, I wondered if she had found a way to sneak into a pod. Perhaps someone was helping her? But who would do that? No adult would do that, so she must be lost deep in the building somewhere.

Was she eating? Was she doing OK? I reached out my hand – just a fraction, in the mirror less than a millimetre, but within my body, I reached out the whole way, into a corner. I closed and opened my hand so that she might, somewhere, feel that I was holding her hand.

But of course she was at home, helping along with her brother, helping the family get through the absence. The true absence, which was me, of course, I had left them again. I want to explain how I experienced all this, but I find that I can't.

I was glad to have a long, hot shower. I polished myself. I felt as though I had actually shed a whole skin. The skin that had lost its daughter, that had felt her vanish into thin air, was gone. It was me now. I was just a person at work, with a family out there doing their thing, and I was going to be fine.

As I have said, we were in the changing rooms after our showers. There were four colleagues in there.

'What even is this place?' I said.

'Accommodation,' said a guy who was vigorously drying himself.

'How long have you been here?' I asked. 'How many nights?'

He just looked at me, with his naked body and all his hair.

[A voice: **Are you feeling all right? You've stopped moving I think.**]

I am struggling a little bit to breathe actually. Could you give me just a moment?

[A voice: **Can I get you some water? Would you like me to change that dressing?**]

Thank you, no.

Thank you.

It has passed. The feeling of panic moves away. I can't explain it. I found myself being invited to a new meeting, a new project. We walked from the shower rooms directly to the collaboration area and I began mapping out content strategies for new strands of Capmeadow expansion work. I spent a long time just sitting on a comfortable chair. I felt the day come on – I believe I contributed to several important discussions about language within the new Capmeadow estate. Space, I was asked a lot about the way we can describe space that would not feel alienating to those with 'legacy' concepts of space. Where you actually are, I kept saying. It's about where you actually are, and I remember spending an entire team dinner being told that this was both correct and incorrect.

I remember the smile of the colleague who said this to me. I don't remember his name. He floated behind a candle. The restaurant where we had the team dinner was a kind of French brasserie. There were others at the table. At a certain point I stopped and looked around because I thought I heard my daughter laughing. I looked out at the darkness of the night. I didn't question how this restaurant had come to be there in our business park. I didn't seem able to ask anything, but could only speak very fast. I seemed to take a kind of psychological run-up, and then acceptance. I entered the period of acceptance. I don't know if you remember the period of acceptance, or if this was just something I created for a specific team, but we were all in it for a while. I produced training material for the period of acceptance.

Transcribed footage #2:
Tom Crowley in various locations

1. Daytime, in a busy hub in the central area of Capmeadow. Tom walks through the groups of professionals who have gathered for informal meetings. In the footage, you can see the erasure lines where some of these people are clutching the sides of their heads or lying down on the ground. There is a sense of order to everything that feels completely natural, and yet it is clearly an editorial trick. Only Tom Crowley's expression seems genuine. He moves carefully around the erased shapes of people, not wanting to disturb them, sensing that they must need their own space, and yet checking them. Yes, he is checking them to see if they are his daughter. He checks all of the people he sees. It's a micro-action, barely noticeable unless you have been tracking his movements.

2. Tom Crowley enters a café and buys coffee and a croissant. He sits at a table and talks again; in that low, soft voice, he's more audible here. He is talking about shoes. He's talking as if he's telling someone a story, but it's a boring

story about shoes. I need new shoes, Hen, he is saying. I need something more comfortable. It's very painful all this walking. I got you a croissant, look. He continues talking in this way for some time, and his words, though soothing, are cracked with a sort of emotional strain, as though he has learnt what will and will not be detected, if that's the right term, by the Capmeadow archival system.* He talks about shoes, he talks to his daughter about shoes and a shop he will go to for them. There's a hiking shop, he says. Isn't that ridiculous, but we do go hiking, some of us. I am joining the hiking club, so I can try and spot you out there. I think you do this too. I think you too are walking every day. He leaves the croissant. He watches the table from outside, through the café window. A shadow moves across the screen. The croissant is gone. Tom Crowley too has moved on and is walking in the

---

* **Archivist's note:** In fact, I wonder now if those shoals of fish in the coolant waters have something to do with this? What else are they eating if not this essence? They nose at things, disturbances, they check for signs of irregularity and gradually erode the irregularities away from existence. Does that make sense? Would you feel it, inside the archive? Would it cause a reaction to the skin of an archived image, to be grazed on by a pale white fish, floating in there with your data? Perhaps it is not limited to the fish. What am I eating? I snack. I have eaten many pastries, I feel like. I can taste the fat and the final sweetness. What is the significance of this? What did I last snack on? There's a hatch. There's a bathroom. I find myself heading for the corners for everything, The hatch in one corner of the room. The bathroom door in another. I do not recall the last time I ate. I do not recall the last time I went to the bathroom. I lie in my bed. I dream of these two people. I try to imagine how it would feel to live without this ache I have, the ache in my stomach, in my jaw, behind my eyes, always there, a worry. I wonder what I would see if I climbed out of the archive now. Would any of it be there? I dream of mist and everything succumbing to the mist.

square, continuing to talk about shoes, and about how important it is to stay hydrated, to eat a balanced diet, and to be true to yourself, and never let anyone tell you you're not good enough, or that you don't exist, or that you're not here. You're here, he keeps saying, and I am here too.*

3. Tom Crowley in a meeting in the open-air co-working spaces on West Green (known previously as Site G, Midwest Point, Hazel Grove, Modern Area 2 and others – also, previously does not mean previously in time, but previously in my experience of seeing it within my work in the archive. Even the shape of this measure of time is difficult for me to track). He is approached by Cath Corbett, who attempts to join the meeting, but is struck by a sense of not being here. Cath Corbett is standing and talking with the others, but the managers talk around her, addressing Tom directly. This footage shows Cath Corbett is already in doubt not just of herself, but of her lasting presence in the archive. She is flattened in some frames, part grass, part picnic table. The sun ignores her. Cath has no shadow. She comes back together only when someone says her name.

---

* **Archivist's note:** And I too am here. I am here.

Rare complete fragment relating to Tom Crowley's practical work

The business park is expanding. Come with us to the NuYu peace gardens (at the rear of Building 3) to discuss what this means for you and your role here. It's an exciting time to be part of the Capmeadow family. Your complimentary lunch will be provided. To receive the correct lunch, please complete the following questionnaire.

* **Archivist's note:** He does all this rushing around. He obsesses me, this strange little man, and yet his actual work, his product, is really just nothing. What even is this? What value does it add? It makes me sadder than anything else to look at this little note he has written, and to think of the feelings in his body, and his mind, as he strains to produce these things. After all of this, his actual labour is not even of a high quality.

Cath Corbett speaks

Ah, OK, I sit here then? This is a nice seat. Well, thanks for seeing me.

[A voice: That's what I'm here for. Thank *you* for coming.]

I like the way you welcome people. I am Cath Corbett. I've been with the firm for a few years. Is that relevant? I suppose everything is, right?

[A voice: Yes, you can talk about anything you like. I will pass along your feedback.]

God – do you know, I sounded just like him then. Did you know that?

[A voice: Just like who?]

Oh, this man. Sorry, I did explain in my email that I wanted to talk about a specific person. Tom Crowley I mean. He works for me – when he can be tracked down, that is. When he can be made to actually sit and *do* some work. Right?

Ugh. Right? I keep saying Right? Like he does. It's enraging. I have no idea when it started. He's been undermining me. Permeating me. My words.

[A voice: Permeating your words?]

So – for example, he might be writing a questionnaire for me, and he will ask questions about what he is meant to be doing, and every sentence, right? He says 'right?' at the end. Like this:

'And the questionnaire is in the link, right?'

Right? It's maddening isn't it?

What annoys me the most is that every single time, without fail, he'll be saying something so fucking obvious that he must know – like *must always knowww*. He's got nothing to ask. He already knows. It doesn't need confirming.

'So, and the grass is green, right?' Like that! Jesus I'm angry just thinking about him.

I know it sounds like a small issue, but he really really does my head in with it. Don't get me wrong, his actual work, when he does it, is pretty good. He also does – or rather used to do – ad hoc stuff for me whenever I asked, which was useful. He was sort of kind.

I feel bad really, I know he's obviously had some kind of breakdown there. Or at least that's how it looks. He turned up one day with his daughter, then starts telling everyone he's lost her. It turns out he took her home, and just forgot. Or something. She might not have been there. Anyway – he was still the only content specialist I had available, so he was writing emails for me. He should've taken time off, but he kept working. Although, I do actually understand him wanting to keep working because a lot of us felt like this expansion must be coming at a cost. It seemed obvious that some people would end up getting sacked. Nobody wanted to get sacked. I was losing sleep over the idea of not working here, even though the cost to me personally of continuing to work here has been immense.

A few people did get sacked of course, but not as many as I thought it would be. Not that I paid much attention – during those early days, it felt like if you weren't part of the expansion project, you were nothing. So I stuck to it like glue. I took on extra work even – whenever something was needed for the expansion project, I leapt at it. I brought Tom along with me. He'll never admit that he owes me for that.

But you asked me about that lunch, didn't you?

[A voice: No, I don't think so. Which lunch is this?]

We had to do some comms regarding the new canteen in what was, back then, Capmeadow C. The first new building. I remember because he did that annoying thing asking 'right' at the end of the sentence.

'And these lunches, they're somehow specialised, right?' Like that.

'Yeah, that's right,' I said. 'Just like I explained.'

'So I don't need to change anything?'

'No, Tom, what you've written is fine really.'

And there was this questionnaire, that I had explained to him about a thousand times I was dealing with. But Tom says,

'OK, so what about the questionnaire? I leave that to you, right?'

I told him again, yes, I handle the questionnaire.

He was very keen to attend the lunch himself, even though it was actually not for us to attend.

'I think it will help with my work on these expansion events,' he said. But you could tell he was lying. I told him it wouldn't be appropriate for him to attend this lunch, but when the day came, he was there. He was dressed up a bit, but nowhere near the level – like *nowhere near* the level you needed to be dressed.

I had to follow him around the whole time because he kept talking to the senior managers. He was creeping around peering into corners. Trying to find her – that's what he was doing. Nobody else noticed it, but I saw. I saw him talking out of the corner of his mouth. He thought his daughter was still lost somewhere. Insane.

You know, but not the kind of insane that you keep to yourself. Not the normal kind of insane, where the company will support you, and you can have the time off you need, and everyone sends you a card, and you can return to light duties. Do you remember light duties? There used to be light duties and now look at us.

But with him, it was spreading. It came off him like butter, covering everything he touched. I blame him, I'm not alone, right? A few of us have noticed that it was his chaos that started all this. Are you recording this?

[**A voice: As I have said, everything we say here is captured and sent along to the central database.**]

Right, good. I want it recorded. He did something. He *did* something.

[**A voice: I'm not sure what you mean. You were talking about lunch?**]

OK, fine, yes. So on that lunch day, he had taken someone else's lunchpack, which caused chaos. Well, not chaos, we sorted it out, but the whole point of those lunchpacks is that they are created according to the exact needs of an individual. It's all in the data. The lunchpack was the whole point of the event. These things, you know, it's not even real food, like you would normally get. It's not like noodles in the precinct or curry at Wallahs! – right?*

[**A voice: Would you like some water?**]

No! Fucksake. What was I saying?

[**A voice: You were talking about lunchpacks.**]

Right, that's right. You can't just eat any old person's lunchpack!

---

* **Archivist's note:** At this use of the word 'right?' at the end of the sentence, Cath Corbett looks physically sick. She reduces visibly.

The new Capmeadow learns what you want for lunch, that's what we were saying. No – not what you want – what you *will* want. I had that argument with him too. The more I think about him, the more I feel like he was the one who started all this. I know you won't accept that anything is happening, but of course it is, and of course it can't be all his fault, but I blame him. I'd like to kill him. I'd like to *kill him*.

[A voice: OK. Is there another way you can say how you feel, do you think? With new words, perhaps. We can't continue here if you're talking about killing people. I'll have to stop the meeting. Can you try?]

I'll try. OK. I'll try.

At home, I used to have a wardrobe. OK? It was a vintage piece with four doors, all in a row. Perfect for two people who love their clothes. Each door had a key. The keys were all identical. I had this boyfriend. Partner or whatever. He lived with me for a while, and he had one door of the wardrobe for himself. Just one door, obviously, because it was my house, and he hadn't committed to fully moving in, and spent one half of every month in his old family home, looking after his sister who had a neurological issue. Anyway, he has one door, I have three doors. They're all the same. And until he moved in, they all worked fine.

Now, this man, my partner, he was lovely. The love of my life really. Soft and daft, but never ever unhappy. He made me feel so safe, and I know I did the same for him. Because he was not a confident man. He was all right most of the time, but he was prone to these sudden lapses in confidence. It would just leave him in a split second.

Sometimes, when he tried to open his side of the wardrobe, he might have a lapse, just as he was turning the key. He'd lose his way somewhere in the rotation of the key. Maybe once or twice a month this would happen, and he seemed to turn the key in a strange way. Not roughly, but somehow without conviction. His frail way of turning the key would lead it to jam. The door could not be opened. Broken, broken. You had to leave it a few hours and then go back and open it with confidence. He would cry over it. Sometimes, he'd be late for work and there'd be nothing we could do. He'd sit on the bed and hold his head in his hands. Of course, he was crying for his sister who was still so young, and had years left to live, but would never get better, and would never become the woman – the remarkable woman – he had always known she would become. But also for himself. He cried because it would place him, this lapse, this strange key turn, it would place him in the low part of the world. A low-impact life. A nothing man. All completely unfair and untrue, because he was wonderful and caring and really, even crying there in his wet towel in the damp room, with all his folds, he was very beautiful. To me he was, even his white back.

But that didn't matter. It never mattered how wonderful he was, or how much I was struck by his very heavy beauty, it didn't matter, he was inconsolable. And the wardrobe, a physical object, that too became inconsolable. And I would not be able to shake it even from myself. The room sagged under it. The house and the street outside became momentarily desolate because of my partner's sadness. The other houses looked grim. Spiteful faces looked down from their windows. I had to go round the house clapping my hands. Putting music on. Showing him it was all right. But that was just a house, and my partner with his big moon-shaped body in the towel.

My theory is that Tom, this guy, Tom, he is like my ex-partner but somehow super-amplified. He came in here with his weird breakdown – a total cataclysmic failure of confidence – and now everything has gone to shit. I'm not supposed to swear, but I haven't seen that wardrobe, for example, for years now.

[A voice: **Do you think it's possible you have your timelines wrong there? The expansion project is still in its primary stages.**]

I tell you, I have not seen anything except this corridor for years. Can you understand me? I'm sitting on the carpet. That is not a metaphor, right?

[A voice: **I'm sorry, you're saying a corridor?**]

Yes. I worked late after that man's daughter *didn't* go missing. And I wanted to find a toilet. I went looking but everywhere was locked on the floor where I was sitting. So I went down, out to the back of B building, down into the basement where the auditorium was. And I opened the black doors that led to the toilet.

I began to worry I was getting lost because the corridor was so dark beyond the pooled lights, like pebbles of gold every few feet, the rest so lightlessly black. The carpet made no sound at all. I believe I arrived at the toilet. I have a memory of backlit mirrors and a great deal of copper and patinaed surfaces, fragrances like eucalyptus and pine, but nice, not shit like that sounds, not like a car freshener like that sounds when I say it, but somehow the actual deepest meaning of eucalyptus and pine. I remember feeling like it was the most luxurious late-night work poo anyone anywhere has ever done. But I don't remember leaving. I don't remember anything else, except being in the corridor.

And if I lose my focus, I am back there. I'm there now. The corridor aligns to the building, of course, so it's fine while I am in the office, and I can go out into the grounds.

[A voice: **It's wonderful out in the grounds. This is an essential part of the expansion project.**]

But I cannot go home. I sleep here.

I've heard they are building accommodation up on the ridge now, so I will probably take a chalet. Are there ridge chalets available? I deserve something. I *deserve something*. And actually, that's what I came to talk to you about – how do I tell you what kind of décor I want?

I saw AJ Cotten's dwelling in the latest edition of the brochure, and I don't think it's fair at all. Like, how did she get that place? And also – how did she get that feature in the fucking brochure? *I used to be responsible for all brochure content*, and I wasn't made aware at all of this change. Who edits the brochure nowadays? You'll have to email me or something if you don't know off the top of your head. Message it to me, right? Fuck. Message it to me, because I can no longer use the staff directory.

[A voice makes as if to speak, but only gets as far as drawing a breath.]

But you know who I mean, right? That Tom guy. You know who he is at least? Admit that, you have to admit that. Because sometimes people pretend they don't remember that guy. They pretend not to notice any of what's going on here. I had to walk for half an hour to get to this room, did you know that? Where has all of this come from? It's fucked is what it is. *I want to kill someone.* I realise that sounds extreme, but I do imagine it a lot of the time.

[A voice: Would you like to talk about having dark thoughts?]

I'm on the carpet. I am absolutely on the carpet.

[A voice: Some water maybe?]

I don't want any fucking water.

Transcribed footage #3: Cath Corbett is treated badly. She reacts in an understandable way

1. Footage of Cath Corbett and Tom Crowley in discussion. They are walking down one of the main streets in the heart of Capmeadow. Everything is well established here, but still there are mounds of refresh and replenish material growing up in certain gaps. In other places, buildings are in the process of being degenerated. Wires emerge from windows in some buildings, clustered like tentacles. Cath is gripping Tom's arm. She is angry with him. Her words are mangled by the ageing of the footage, but it's clear she is blaming Tom Crowley for somehow causing whatever it is that's happened in her workplace since the day he brought his daughter to work (though of course in fact, as we have established, he did not bring her – although that sort of seems to be the point of what Cath is saying).

2. Cath Corbett alone in the streets at night. This is in the region of Capmeadow where she has been allocated

a chalet. She stands on the black surface of the road and looks up at the moon. She is singing, very gently, a love song. It's impossible to make out the words. She is swaying slightly. She shouts the words up to the sky; her face opens in a smile. She seems briefly to be somewhere else. She looks as though she is being held, in an embrace with an invisible figure. She looks happy, her face is curved into a gleeful smile, an absence overtakes her eyes. She is completely uninhibited, she is dancing to music that only she can hear. The music that is often played in these streets stops at the time the sun sets, so there is definitely no sound. A group of colleagues walk past, they seem happy to see her. One of them, a woman in a cocktail dress, dances with her. Respectfully, out of empathy, she dances with her. Keeps her company. The others all do the same, in varying degrees of sincerity. Some of the other dancers are not confident. When Cath Corbett eventually shudders and begins to cry, the group gather themselves and move on. Across the road from where Cath Corbett is sitting, she sees a sign. It's one of the signs created by Tom Crowley. It's not clear what the message says from the screen, but Cath Corbett stands in front of it for a long time and does not move.

3. Cath Corbett starts to be seen with a group of employees who cover their faces in public. They are not regulation face coverings, such as provided for in the equalities policy of the regulated Capmeadow space. I have seen this document, I have learnt it, I think. I know many codes, but I don't always know which code supersedes other codes. I should say, these last few words are not part of the transcript. These are ski masks, or other winter

gear. Not banned, of course, but strange. It's strange. Cath Corbett and the others meet in strange locations where they think they will not be disturbed. In each other's dwellings. During legitimate team meetings. They meet in the park of the silver rabbits, during the time when the silver rabbits were deployed there. This period is, I think, not just a single period of time, but a regular occurrence. They meet briefly. They disperse in a choreographed way. Cath Corbett meets regularly with the Liaison Officer (also referred to as A voice in this archive) – first in their original office, and then in the museum setting. Each time Cath Corbett attends these meetings, she appears to switch between states of managerial directness and tremendous pain. Cath Corbett's decline shames us all – this is not visible in the footage, so this breaks the rules of transcription, but this is the overwhelming feeling that you get as you watch Cath Corbett, and I think if it is still possible, and if anyone reads these notes, outside of archival interest, and if there is still time, then Cath Corbett should be given help. She should be supported. I do not feel that this message will be heard. Cath Corbett stands alone in a road; she looks incredibly small and incredibly, unbearably tired.

4. Cath Corbett enters the museum; she explores the many galleries with an expression of yearning on her face. She sees Tom Crowley in one of the main galleries. He is examining something on the wall. She avoids him. She seems furious.

5. A different place, further out. The mound has grown fully now into a double chalet building. Nearby is a

coffee stall. The sky is heavy with its blueness. A blue forcing itself down into the spaces of the park, pushing against the green fibres and lawns that spread across the surface. The figure of Tom Crowley emerges from a misted area. He's walking the limit of the park. He can be seen from camera to camera, sensor to sensor, treading the line where the park ends and the outer world, presumably, continues. Nothing of this further place is revealed. It's just where another town is, probably – or some say it's more unused land that has been procured by the Capmeadow Territory Group, which is mentioned several times in multiple places in meeting minutes, though each time it has a different function, or there is a variation on its name. Whatever that land is, it remains unseen, unheard, and is forced out of the mind (I will forget about it within the next few seconds). Tom Crowley is talking as he walks; his words are crisp to the ear, but do not translate into meaningful speech in the archive. Only his tone comes through, in noises and pitches that remind me of hearing a story being read. A voice of comfort, maybe, the natural voice of comfort. I have fallen asleep many times listening to the voices of people like Tom Crowley, who is walking alone, speaking to someone who isn't there.*

6. Tom Crowley leaves an office cluster where he has been working. The yellow light around him makes him just a shadow as he passes the windows where other employees continue their meetings, pressing through the delivery

---

* **Archivist's note:** Although I am here. I listen maybe when nobody else can. I reply, too, of course, in sounds. In noises.

cycle. Tom has his hands in his jacket pocket. He walks carelessly, he seems to be whistling. From time to time he takes his hand out of his coat pocket and makes the crab-claw gesture. He does not notice that he is being followed by Cath Corbett and a group of other employees. They shout at him, but the audio does not work correctly. I find it difficult to watch this sequence. Tom is not a fast runner. The gang catches up with him, there is a struggle, Tom frees himself, but is limping. The gang approaches again. This time one of them swings something at Tom's head. It catches him badly; he limps and keeps trying to run, but soon they are on him. It is too much to watch this sequence. I cannot coldly report what needs to be reported. I see him look up at the camera, just one eye, peering out from under the blows and kicks that rain down upon him. I see him look and remember who might see him, and he smiles. He tries to say, I am sure, don't worry about me. Don't worry, I am fine. This will be over soon. It goes on for such a long time. The gang members, with Cath Corbett looking on, take it in turns to punch or kick him. Tom doesn't move any more. He is curled on the floor. He covers his face with his arms.

7. Tom Crowley is using a public workspace to make a video call to his family. He is badly bruised, his face is swollen, he seems only able to move one of his arms. But he is smiling as he talks to them on the screen. He keeps saying, it seems, I am OK! It was nothing! A silly event. He keeps on saying things that are just on the surface of connection. The faces of his family do not have expressions on the screen. Even when frozen, even when enhanced and enlarged, even here in this archive room

where I have access to the best possible screens with the highest imaginable resolution, there is nothing to see on the faces of the family that Tom Crowley is addressing. It's hard to watch, almost as hard as when he is being beaten in the street, or spat on, or abused verbally, all by groups of people who seem to blame him for causing whatever they think the problem is. The faces of his family are smooth, like brown eggs.

Tom Crowley continues speaking

I threw myself into the job. As part of the expansion project team, I soon found I had a more and more receptive audience. My signs were taken seriously.

[A voice: Would I have seen these signs?]

Yes, of course, they're in constant use and constant refinement. At first the requirements came through Cath Corbett, who used to be my dotted-line line manager, but there was a problem with her health, I think, she had some issues with location, she said. I don't really know the full story to be honest. In the meetings about this, Cath would glare at me and seem to be in immense pain. She had these headaches, that's what she said. And other things, she said other things that were highly disturbing. She reported that she was trapped somewhere. Something had happened and she was summoned (her word) against her will to be here when in fact she was in dire need of rescuing from somewhere, she was stuck in a mistaken piece of architecture. It sounded plausible, but also, no matter how much I might have thought I wanted to help her, the whole thing repulsed me. It repulsed us all. Cath Corbett would sort of writhe around. Have you ever seen that?

Sometimes someone starts writhing around and screaming? I have seen it, and I try not to let it worry me. The feeling comes and goes. When Cath Corbett last did this, I literally talked over her, and eventually she composed herself. If you ever do see anything like this, you have to just do your best to stay yourself. You can't help that person. You taught me that, I think. Or your team did. I think those messages came from here. Isn't that funny? I have done work for you, writing reassurances for writhing and screaming incidents. Procedures were drafted by someone, and I had to extract meaningful training from them. I feel like that was you. I have been thinking more and more that it was you.

Anyway, Cath's leadership was in question. The headaches and the other things showed no sign of getting better, and any time she tried to speak to a doctor, she told me the whole experience would make her feel increasingly sad and despondent. I don't know. I feel bad about Cath Corbett, looking back, but also what could I have done? She was never supportive of me, of course. And was one of the many people who looked askance after I lost my daughter on Bring Your Daughter to Work Day. Which I officially still agree never happened.

In fact, the way Cath Corbett presented in those feedback meetings became the foundation for new warnings. She would be trying to give me notes or raise new items for the agenda, and the rest of the stakeholders present would be nodding on their screens or in the room, but meanwhile, in the sidebar chat, the private channels in which Cath Corbett was not present, someone else would be typing—

'She's losing it completely. We need to warn against *exactly* this negative attitude. Please send me direct ideas etc.'

'Yes, ideally we can use her as a source of what to warn against. Just keep her talking.'

'Oh Jesus, is she writhing?'

'Tom, we urgently need anti-writhing encouragement.'

And so I was given a wider brief – specifically, how to combat writhing – which we agreed could not be the business name for it, and so we settled for overwhelmedness and phantomist headaches.

I never really met the people making these requests. I would just check their seniority and agree to do whatever they wanted, and then I would join meetings with their representatives. It happened all the time. I was happy to do it because it meant more access. More access meant more chances to look for Hen: in flagrant breach of everything that was logical, I still looked for her. I was letting everything else happen.

At home, the family sealed itself over my absence; I represented a sort of painless wound, that's how it seemed, and they didn't like thinking about me. I talked to them, to the children, to my wife, but nothing stuck. I was in there, but did not belong. I am there now, probably, in some way. We're not supposed to talk like this, and I can see it upsets you to imagine too much in that direction, but I'm used to it. I am there and here. Maybe. Maybe I'm not there.

When I was in the middle of a discussion with one of the designers last week, to talk about sizing of subtitle copy, I was also in my living room. There were official-looking people there, they had come to the house. Someone sat in a chair, with their hands covering their face. It was me. I was the one with my hands covering my face. It was because of a sad phone call, I was taking a very sad phone call, and I was completely numb. My son shouted something as he left the room. I returned to the meeting. We cannot think too much about this here. What would it achieve? At this time, I could only think about being here, in Capmeadow, so that when Hen needed me, she would be able to find me. Or even if she never knew who I was. If I was just a colleague, for example, who just happened to be around and could be asked to perform collegiate tasks.

I was interested only in being spread as wide as I could at work. I was still allowing that sickness to work in me, still allowing myself to hunt for her, to find her before anything happened. What was she eating? Was she looking after her hygiene? Would she have cleaned her teeth? How many days had it been? The number of days would not resolve.

I became a shell, I worked diligently, without rest, without question, without complaint, I became a Capmeadow native. I ignored the fact that I was standing on the stairs, in my home, trying to hear what my son was saying through the walls.

[A voice: Perhaps we should get back to the training material itself? I believe that is something we should talk about if possible.]

Of course. Thank you again for the water, by the way. I'm incredibly thirsty after all the smoke. So, yes, anyway, the warning messages and ad hoc training material requests became far more general. I seemed to be hitting the right note because my remit expanded seemingly every day.

At one point, I worked on an issue being reported where colleagues sometimes had problems if they were *too much with themselves*.

This was the phrase we agreed on, *too much with themselves*, it seemed to work best. We tried several other more medical-sounding phrases: *presenting with symptoms characteristic of detachment*, but the medical advisors told us this was not really helpful, and could lead people to believe they had a real medical condition. So we fell back to more general stuff. The idea I had was, it could be something your nana would say. *He's too much with himself,* was my suggestion. I've never heard my grand-mother, either of my grandmothers, say this, but it's definitely something that they could have said.

What we were trying to capture was the sensation expe-rienced during the initial expansion phase when colleagues would be gripped by panic, or something quieter than panic, but deeply felt.

Things would occur to someone, abstract things, a window in front of them, that should not be there, and the feeling that they should open that window, and lean out, and look for their husband to see if his car was in the drive, but of course, there was no window, there was only the dining table in the new vintage-inspired refectory-cum-mess hall. And this window or whatever it was that had occurred to them would cause a sort of crisis, which in turn would lead to a drop in concentration, and – I can't exactly explain what would happen then, of course, because I too was experiencing this sudden sensation that I was on the stairs, just on the stairs, wondering if it would be possible to rescue the relationship I once had with my son.

But, somehow, I was able to go away and write the messaging, and when I came to present the guidance it seemed to make sense and my stakeholders signed off on it. I was congratulated, in fact. I could not see exactly what I had written.

If you asked me now what the guidance said, I would have trouble remembering. Only a few key phrases stand out, and I want to talk more about them, but not yet. If I can just finish this one point first.

What mattered was, I was given access to absolutely every single area of Capmeadow. In and out of the expansion areas.

Cath Corbett would try to pin me down for meetings, and I would change the location so I could look for my daughter in some new venue. She's going to come around that corner, I would be thinking, and Cath Corbett would be going on about her difficulties accessing management-level resources, and I would be staring at the spaces that go unseen in this place, where you can see the raw material, where it is only partly finished. She will come around that corner, I would hold my breath, refusing to exhale while Cath Corbett fell apart across the table from me.

'We'll have to figure this out on our own,' she said to me in one of the last physical meetings we had together. 'Raul's team have got their claws into the senior expansion committee. If we're not careful they'll cut us loose.'

'But they liked the content,' I said, annoyed that I was forced to breathe, still looking at the corner.

'It doesn't matter that they liked it, you idiot, they're taking the credit!'

I stopped listening. Poor Cath Corbett. I hope you can help her. I don't have the energy for it any more. If I'm honest, I think I am fading completely. I feel my muscles giving way sometimes. I really do wonder how long this day has been. I feel so tired. I sleep. I sleep all the time, but how long has passed? I am grey I think. My teeth are crumbling at the back. I won't show you, but it's bad. And now I think I have a lot of smoke damage. I feel like I need to slow down. I was wondering if I could come and work with you.

I mean, this is why I'm here. I realise, after the fire, I realise you might be reluctant. I don't even know if you're hiring. I've been talking for such a long time. I feel like I've been talking for years. I meant to say, I am really impressed by this place, the museum I mean. What a monument. It's strange that in such a grand building, you have chosen this place as your office. What is this place?* I've looked all through this museum and this is my favourite room by a long way. I feel strangely safe here. I'd be very happy working here I think. What do you think?

You'll think it's ridiculous, but I – I don't know, maybe I am tired, maybe that's why I came to talk to you anyway, maybe because of the fire, I feel strange. I never stopped looking for her. I – I have been looking for so long.

In the early days, I would see her, I mean not exactly her, but traces of her. I would see evidence of her. There would be someone's abandoned lunch – the sandwiches or whatever would have been nibbled in the exact way that Hen would nibble. There was a new café, or a new relaxation space, and I would get there as soon as I could, but she would have just left. There would be bean bags arranged in her exact way. I would go and sit there.

A particular coffee place opened, and I went back again and

---

* **Archivist's note:** The room used by the Liaison Officer (known as A voice in this archive) is in fact a small room inside the museum that looks like a reconstruction of early (pre-expansion) Capmeadow. There are a few tables stacked with piles of unused paper, there are boards with pictures on. Behind where the officer is sitting there are many photographs of smiling children. Throughout this conversation, since he entered the room and began talking, Tom Crowley has been occasionally staring up at this collage of photographs. There are children smiling into the camera, huge blue eyes, and brown eyes, and grey and green eyes. Some of them are wearing hard hats, science lab coats. They look like they're having a good time. I am looking at them now and seeing what I think Tom Crowley is seeing. The little girl must be around eight years old (though don't ask me how I know this because I do not have memories of eight years old); she is sitting at a desk with two friends, smiling but with a reluctance on her face, the smile is not complete. And the sign above her, if I squint, is not quite as obscured as it should be; it says Bring Your Daughter to Work Day 2024.

again to try and see her. She was never there. But something told me she was coming, so I would buy a croissant for her, and leave it on the table untouched, with a little napkin on which I would draw a heart or just a kiss. I know some people noticed this, and I was probably reported because sure enough after a few weeks I was asked to write training material to discourage the purchase and then immediate waste of food. We did a campaign called Energy Level Check or something. We advised people not to accept messages from their brain that they were in starvation mode.

In the end I had to buy the croissants and leave them only briefly while I went to the toilet. Only once did I come back to find it had been eaten, or rather destroyed and partly eaten, with flakes of pastry all over the table. It could have been anyone who ate the croissant. But it was her. It was my daughter, I know it was. No matter how impossible that sounds to you, it was her.

After this croissant, I felt more convinced than ever that she was here. I kept a record, but of course I had to keep it coded, and hid it in plain sight. As work came in for me to write safety information for the continued expansion of the business park, I began to see ways of including messages to my daughter.

There was a period when I worked and sat in the dark space that occupied what we called Point West. It was called Point West because of a bar that had opened there – it had games, like bar games, billiards and skittles and suchlike, I don't know if you're aware of it. I don't know if it's still standing.

[A voice: I do know Point West – it had games of all kinds. Shuffle something, and giant cribbage. Oh I loved that place. Did you used to go there? I feel as though I should have seen you. But perhaps not. Sorry. I'm not meant to talk so much.

I – but it's so interesting because I used to go there all the time.]*

So you do know it? That's good! That's interesting. I would have been in the dark building a few hundred yards away, you may not even have noticed it. It was in there we had a series of crisis meetings about the development of the estate. One thing on everyone's minds was to do with timelines.

'We have a timeline problem, Tom.' This was a new manager talking to me. I had stopped asking their names. This one was called Raul Kunis. He was flanked by more senior managers who nodded as he spoke.

'Is this the issue of the day?' I asked. This was a guess because I wasn't completely sure what the issue of the day really meant. It was something I had seen on agendas of various meetings I was invited to that were described as 'Optional' and so I didn't ever go.

'Yes. The issue of the day. That's what some people are calling it. The issue being we're not sure how long days are lasting at the moment. I mean, everyone is operating fine, the CEO is fine with it, the senior management team are comfortable. But I am sure you've noticed, several of us have had to attend funerals during stand-ups, for example, many of us live in darkness, for example.'

He talked like this, Raul Kunis, he would launch into something that seemed like it had an ending, and then he would be at the funeral of one of his parents, or he would be struggling to lock the doors of his home. He would sweat. At this moment,

---

* **Archivist's note:** It's worth noting that at this moment the owner of 'A voice' is looking very closely at Tom Crowley; she seems to see something there in the space between them that intrigues her. She almost seems to be on the verge of tears.

on the screen, he closed his eyes and began to glisten. But he continued. He understood exactly all of the guidance and warnings I had been producing, and – amazingly – he seemed to be following them. Even as he was sweating and looking like he might throw up, I could see that he was, internally, repeating affirmations that I had produced. He recovered enough to proceed.

'People are anxious, is my point, because the timelines for completing the expansion do not seem to fit into the normal quarterly cycle of delivery that we insist on for most development work. Right?'

'Right.'

'So people are developing products, meeting with clients, we're making things, productivity is in line with expectations, but too many colleagues have lost their sense of where we are in the year. Even to the extent that, and this is where that name came from, we're not sure whether the day has ended yet or a new one has begun.'

He said this casually of course, and I accepted it casually, even though, if you think about it too much, this is an absolutely dizzying concept, isn't it? What day is it? Don't answer that, it won't do you any good. Yes, I will take some water, thank you. Thank you for being so kind, by the way. You're so kind. I'm so proud of you.

[A voice: I'm sorry but that doesn't sound quite right. I think, er, you must have misspoken just now regarding being proud of me, I think we can say we are proud of each other as a community of practice. Is that what you meant? We will assume so.]

I suppose, yes, you're right. I must have meant that. I was also wondering though, do you feel appreciated?

Do people thank you often enough? They should. Are they polite and kind? They should be. They should thank you all day. I am saying it for all of them, and I want to say, also, please keep this going, and keep being yourself, and keep trying – I have seen that you try so very hard. It's wonderful. You should be so proud of this, of all of the things you are doing.

[**A voice: Thank you for saying these nice things. But we should press on.**]

You're right, I should return to what I was saying, but I don't want to. I looked for her. I looked for my daughter and I tried to speak to her – and so some of the messages were just for her, if she was lost, if she felt unsure. Some of the very affirmations that Raul Kunis was saying to himself, internally, were designed for my daughter. They were things like, Focus on your hand. Make the crab claw with your hand. You can hold the hand of one who makes you feel safe whenever you like. The movement is the steadying action, the focus is the comfort. Make the hand. Feel able to accept. See your objectives. Return to purpose and success.

Those last bits were I guess not for Hen. Though, I suppose, here, these things mean something else. Something more like love.

'It doesn't matter what the day situation is,' I said to Raul Kunis.

'No – that's exactly right!'

'Someone loves you anyway.'

'Well, I mean, we can't exactly say that,' said Raul Kunis, but he knew what I meant.

No matter what the time is, I put in the guidance, *you must keep going. Someone is grateful for your contribution.*

They placed my affirmations, I think, in the Point West area first. Like I was speaking directly into the expansion project.

I said, please make sure you are eating enough. And I said, please make sure you stay warm and find a place for yourself, do you remember that one?

A huge sign that said – 'Look after yourself. Stay positive. Keep going. We are here. All of us are here.'

[A voice: Yes, I remember those. All of us are here. I say that to people who come to see me.]

Of course, it was exactly the generic sort of thing that they wanted me to write, but I was speaking to my daughter, I was speaking only to her, and I was trying to tell her to keep safe.

I was sent all over Capmeadow, which was also my idea. I begged Raul Kunis and anyone else I met and was asked to work for to let me travel as widely as I could, so wherever my daughter was, however she was travelling, whatever sustained her, she would see that I was there.

I placed food in every single café and diner that emerged from the mist. I started to talk to her, too. I'd have wonderful conversations, and somehow find myself being answered.

[A voice: Do you mind if I ask you a question? I'd like to know, do you actually think your daughter is really physically here? Because you also said she is at home.]

Yes. Yes, now more than ever, I think she is here.

[A voice: I'm sorry, but I think you're making a mistake. A terrible mistake, I'm afraid.]

Exit interview after a single day in the Capmeadow crèche

I'm not sure what you expect me to say really. I'd appreciate being able to just leave? It was just a much more challenging job than I expected – so firstly, I am a trained childcare specialist. I have spent years training, and I have a lot of experience working with children in school-age summer camp and play settings. There is technically nothing wrong with the setting you have here. I had a good day with the kids, but I will be honest, it felt strange that none of the parents came to collect them. I handed over to another shift? I'm used to making a bond with the parents as well as the children. Well, not a bond. Who bonds with anyone these days? Everything is so shit. I suppose that's the difference between a formal after-school-club setting and a crèche. Well – you call it a crèche here but I feel like someone named it wrong? None of these kids are below the age of eight. This is a drop-in childminder service really, but for some reason these kids aren't at school? I assumed it was because this is a holiday of some kind. Nobody really told me – I heard different versions of why kids of that age were in the workplace. Why they had been brought into the workplace instead of to school.

Anyway, yes, I have explained to Helen – if that's her name, she said it once and then I barely saw her. She looked like she worked in some other part of the company. Definitely wasn't in the crèche manager's office when I went to ask about breaks. There was just a terminal, and someone on the other end of the terminal told me I could take a break – which really I didn't need because all I wanted by that point was to just go home.

The children were fine. Strangely placid actually. I think the sensory walls have something to do with that. At one point I lost – or thought I had lost – a few of the children, but they had in fact been allowed through the sensory wall in the Yellow Room.

I had trouble gaining access to them, and it's lucky that none of the children were in distress. But, as I said, they never seem to be distressed at all. I have found that street dance and singing can be a great way to get kids to loosen up, but when we completed the song and dance routine, they just looked blankly at me, almost as if they thought it had been a test of some kind? They high-fived each other exactly as instructed, and then they looked at me. They looked at me until I felt compelled to tell them they had done a great job.

Who was best? one of them asked.

I said, it's not really about being the best or even being, you know, 'good'. It's about giving it a go. Although when I tried to say, it's about giving it a go, I actually found myself saying 'it's about giving it one hundred per cent'.

It's stuff like that really. I don't talk like that. Why am I talking like that here? I literally want them to give singing any percentage they feel like. I want them to sing how they feel. I don't think any of those children did a single thing based on how they feel today.

No, that's not true, there was a girl. A funny-looking thing, no offence of course, all kids look funny, but this funny-looking girl seemed to be the only one who wasn't enjoying herself. It was her, I was told, who had shown the other kids how to get accepted through the sensory wall in the Yellow Room.

I was there on the other side waiting for a long time, the light was strange. Sometimes it seemed to fade on them, but I realised my eyes were closing. I realised I was exhausted, which is rare for me. I never get tired. I have an incredibly active life, and I don't get tired before my allocated sleep cycle. I have reinvented my life around my sleep cycle – so when I started to lose the light in that room, when I found my eyelids getting heavy, then yes, I suppose that was the first moment I thought – No. Actually I can't do this? I can't do this.

I wouldn't say I checked out mentally at that stage, but I did think it would take something very special for me to continue working here.

Darren, that's my partner, he has done loads of jobs and I take the piss out of him for this, he has had loads of jobs where he turns up in the morning and it's like at a small airport or something, and they told him to get into a pair of overalls and go clean a plane. With a toothbrush. And he did that for about ten minutes and then just thought, fuck this. It's interesting to be up here on a plane wing scrubbing at the little windows maybe for five minutes, but then he got thinking about the plane. About the people who would be sitting on the other side of the window. And if he was somehow trapped on the wing. If he was stuck there and nobody noticed him, and the only time they realised there was a man in overalls with a toothbrush on the wing of the plane, then whoever was sitting in that seat there, that sort of brown old-fashioned seat there, that person wouldn't be able to save his life. They would have to look at him while he froze to death or got killed by debris, or just slipped away, died from lack of oxygen, or fell off. They would look at him die and feel almost nothing. It would be a story they would tell. A man in overalls on the other side of the little circular window in the plane. They might remember how frightened he looked. They might clutch the cardigan sleeve of their colleague and say – Oh Sue! As long as I live, I'll never forget his face! And Darren, my partner, he told me that as he realised they would just watch him die, he saw his own face inside the plane. Not a reflection, but actually himself, sitting in the plane. He was wearing a kind of suit, but with button-up pyjamas somehow for the shirt. He was sitting there in his pyjamas suit looking coldly back at himself and saying, I can't help you, dude. I can't do anything for you at all.

Anyway, Darren quit about ten seconds after that. He just walked out. He didn't even apologise to me or anything because he wasn't earning at that time. I had to respect it, even though it was something I would never do. Just up and quit a job because of a morbid daydream. I mean, things are not good at the moment. Things are really really bad. And work is work. You know? I mean. Work is – you're lucky if you have something. Anything at all. I know that. And I know I'm here and I've done one day in this easy easy job, and I am already quitting, but it's like Darren said, I just can't die like this.

No – I mean, I don't think I am actually going to die. I just – I don't know. Well actually, so, for example: What time is it? Right now, what is the time? Nobody can tell me the bloody time. Because obviously I left all my phone and everything in the little locker you gave me. And – I have no idea how to get back there either, so that's another thing. I mean, where is that reception area? The one with the weird-looking plants? So that's one thing. But also – that isn't even the main point – the main point is – what time is it? How long was I in there? Because I sat for hours watching them. Or I was told it had been hours.

And I ate while I was there. Several times I ate, sitting looking at them on the other side of that sensory wall.

When I finally discovered the area of the sensory wall through which they had been accepted, I tried to gain acceptance myself, but I didn't – I still don't – know how to do it. I mean there was absolutely no training for any of this. It's not safe to have equipment of this kind that adults cannot operate while children can. They were in this – space, I suppose, a kind of additional room that was also part of the sensory wall. They were behind an amber membrane, and this one girl, she was sort of bossing all the other kids about. And two other girls were with her as sort of support really. Deputising. I am sure the power dynamic in that relationship shifted and changed over time, but that's not the main issue. Like really, it was only her that the sensory – ugh, recess I suppose you'd have to call it – the sensory recess responded only to her. I realised after watching that she was actually the one who had made the sensory wall accept them all in there.

And I was watching them do a sort of domestic scene, except not domestic, not at all domestic, now that I think about it, what they were doing was very kind of work-based play. Each of them had a stuffed toy, just one, those ones with massive eyes. And the little girl was holding her toy very tightly, and telling the others how incredibly stressed she was. And they were explaining that they too were incredibly, unbelievably stressed, they kept saying bloody hell why I can't I focus? Why can't I focus for just ten seconds? And there were some pretend mushrooms and they all said we should eat lion's mane in order to improve our focus. And so they fed each other lion's mane although of course it was just some bits of air, I really must reiterate I didn't allow any of the children in my care to ingest real lion's mane either in mushroom form or as capsules. But they ate the pretend lion's mane and then they said they still couldn't work. How can I work with this screaming going on! That's one of them. I couldn't say which one, but it was obvious that she meant an internal screaming. And I thought – hey that's actually true. How is it that I never noticed this before – so this was the second time I realised that this role, this job rather – is absolutely not for me. Because what IS that screaming sound that seems to be there the whole time? Have you noticed it? A kind of endless roaring sound and those kids just go around in there with this sound in their heads. And they play in amongst it. And for however long – I don't know how long it was – I watched them. I fell asleep several times, and every time I jerked awake, you know, bleurgh – when you've just nodded off and you jerk awake – bleurgh! And they were all still in there. Occasionally one of them would catch my eye and I'd nod at them and say something like – it's nearly time to come out of there, kids. All of my training had sort of deserted me. I just saw them on the other side of the amber membrane, and there was really nothing I could do except watch them. I was completely helpless honestly.

I don't think I said this out loud, but maybe I did, I think it was while I was in one of those dozes, where I said – you won't help me if I am dying. You will just watch me if I am dying. And then I said, in my dream, I hasten to add, not in real life, because I would never say it to a child, but then I said, I also would just watch you die. There is nothing I could do if you were to die now on the other side of the amber membrane. I am feeling incredibly tired now. Listen, I realise I am quitting after just one day, but would it be possible to use the overnight accommodation you promised me? Just once? I would appreciate a place to lie down and try to sleep, just to try and forget all about today, you know? I would love to just forget all about all of it.

A voice speaks about the museum

Delighted to report that I have been asked to move my office into one of the public spaces in the museum. It's a bright space with typical Capmeadow cloud-forestry visible in the distance through the window. My desk is favourably positioned within the space, and I can hear the sounds of the water feature in the grand lobby.

As I'm sure you know, the temporary mist space I encountered and reported to you last time we spoke has been cleared – my thanks to the team for this. Thank you also for vetting my visitors, by the way, if that was you. I already know you won't tell me anything I'm not permitted to know, but I was getting a little bit out of my depth in some of those situations. I am very pleased to report that I hear a lot less talk of being trapped in corridors and so on. It was becoming a bit distracting because I really didn't know what people meant when they said, for example, that they are actually in another room, in another place, and they – I don't know – are bathing their children, but in fact they are standing right in front of me. I think some people have found it easier than others to settle into the expansion of Capmeadow.

Since moving to the museum, though, things have really been improving. Amber came to see me last week – it has been a long time since she and I spent time together. We seem to be getting close to a great friendship, and I wanted to move that forward, so I invited her to come to the museum.

There are several new exhibits – including some references to the establishment of an archive for Capmeadow. There is no physical space yet for the archive, but there is a tremendous sense of depth to the museum structure. The lift, for example, has several basements. Last check showed a basement level of minus twelve. I've gone down as far as minus eight, but the doors don't open.*

Amber met me in the museum café, the main one, that is, not the evening dining tapas experience that serves from 6 p.m. on Wednesday, Thursday, Friday and Saturday only (which I love and have been meaning to take a large party to). We chatted there in the café for a while, and I told her about my new office, I told her about my slightly disastrous date with – with – I've actually forgotten his name now. But I told her about it. That's strange, to have forgotten his name. I remembered it when I told Amber, but I've lost it now. Embarrassing. But I told you about it. I haven't seen him again since then. I remember an angry, desperate face – it's strange, I remember him being in the mist with me and then gone. I—

---

* **Archivist's note:** I remember being asked to join the archiving team and being brought down here in the lift. I remember I was wearing my best clothes. I remember how stiff my shoes were. I remember the plummeting descent. I remember a name, a voice, Jason, something like that. Jason is waiting for me. Jason is supposed to come and check on me. It is very cold down here. Am I down here? Is this down? I could leave the room and check, but I cannot stop watching them. Each fragment comes, and as it passes, I know I will see more of them. My job is surely not meant to make me feel this sad.

So many people seem to come and go at the moment. It's a period of great and exciting change, for sure.

Amber was such good company. After we had talked for a while, she asked me to give her a tour around the museum. It hadn't occurred to me until that moment that I could give tours of the museum! I told her I would be delighted.

Amber, by the way, has very dark black hair, and it seems to colour to blue in the lights of the museum. This was the first exhibit in a way, Amber's hair. We examined the shimmering blue that came out under the black overtones.

As we walked through the display halls, Amber told me about her background. She joined after the first phase of the expansion, she told me. She described a few moments from her childhood – she went to a school in the village where her grandmother lived. Everything in this moment of her life, she told me, was touched with safe and vibrant colours. Like that bright almost turquoise green you get on certain china plates. Amber was able to describe these greens on the walls of her grandmother's house, and in the garden a kind of pink brown on the fences. It was like a painting. She can remember standing in the kitchen and crying because the colours overwhelmed her. And then, after crying, she was wrapped in a little shawl and taken out to the allotment with her grandmother and the allotment people (as they were known). She drank hot squash. It was so sweet it made her mouth itch. We discussed this for a long time. We walked for about an hour through the halls of the museum, and we saw things that are not easy to explain, fantastic things, indescribable things, but all I can really hold on to, all I want to talk about, is this hot squash that Amber used to drink, how the weird sugar replacement in the cordial would pull on the skin on the inside of her mouth and make her head ache, and yet how much she loved it. They had a firepit, she told me, at the allotment.

She told me also, with wild gaps and inconsistencies that I did not stop her to question, about going to the post office on her bike, and the cold in her knuckles. About her grandmother's cupboard full of creams and ointments. About the envelope that would contain her pension money, collected from the post office, that she sprinkled like lavender in the village shops.

Knitted bags, twisted apple trees, that green too, apple green, and gooseberries which she found ugly but addictive to eat.

Her grandmother took her everywhere with her. Amber did not know where her parents had been at this time, but one day they came to collect her and take her back to the town where they lived.

As she told me about this painful experience, of being wrenched from the loving home of her grandmother, we looked at the pale shapes in the corridor.

Before I had shown them to Amber, those shapes (like sculptures but not actually sculpted) had been pleasant, but at a distance from me. I had stood in front of them but felt unmoved. That was before I showed them to Amber, but now, with Amber standing so close to me, and in the context of her grandmother, I found them to make much more sense. They were obviously relics of our childhoods, they were obviously vessels of understanding.

We stood in front of one particular exhibit for a long time. The curves and the dark material of the object felt important, and we stood in silence. I could hear Amber breathing rather shakily. The object slowly resembled something – like figures almost. I was about to say that it looked like us – like me and Amber. But even as I was about to say it, I realised that there were three figures here. Not two. And I felt that same sense of shaking that Amber seemed to. I did not say anything about it. But I remember it now like something cold. Made of metal and glass, or seeming to be made of metal and glass, but easily it could be a liquid. This feeling could be a cold dark liquid.

We moved to another room. I decided to take Amber's hand in my hand. It felt like a natural thing to do. A way of not getting lost. The exhibits did not have labels in that room, but were presented as expressions, perhaps, of the idea of expansion. The size of the hall really amazed Amber. It's true that the space in that hall is pretty substantial. I was more moved, more shocked and happy, when she squeezed my hand.

'It's beautiful,' she said. We continued holding hands for a while as we walked around. I realised how much easier it is for some people to relax here, and how much more at ease I feel with people like Amber than I do with some of the other ones who come to see me with their problems. They seem so lost sometimes, it's draining. And I think you would say that, of course, I only see people when they are in need of consolation. I don't see the everyday happy souls that normally inhabit this workplace, of course. I agree of course of course that's true. But. But also, there are some senseless acts too.

For example, in the gardens of the museum, the beautiful Resilience Garden, do you know it? Of course you know it, but I don't know if you have actually been there. (As I mentioned before, I don't actually know who you are, or if this is an empty room that I come to speak in, I'm sure that somewhere you are listening, just like I have to listen – I am peering into the darkness in the far end of the room. Are you there? No, I think not, but I know you are somewhere, and this is a method of some kind, and I believe in it.)

So, in the Resilience Garden, as I was saying, new architectural forms have been recently added. Silver animals, bronze representations of fruit and flowers. It's the kind of place you can hardly believe exists in a business park. I have been there in the earliest parts of the day, I have walked its limit, and I can tell you it is a wonderful place. But, as you may also know, some people have tried to damage the silver animals. Especially the rabbits there. I found several carved inscriptions with dreadful language in them.

It's a shame isn't it, that's all. A shame to see signs of desperation, in such a tranquil place.

I took Amber there. We lost hours together. I felt like I talked about myself a lot, but I can't remember much of it. Maybe we were just saying stupid things, and then laughing. If I try and explain it, you won't understand. Repeating it would make it lose its quality. I can only tell you that I felt rich. I felt textured. My stomach hurt from laughing. I cooled my face on one of the untouched silver rabbits. I bought tea from a circular cabin. I felt safe and alive, and as we walked back I tried to talk to Amber about myself.

She asked me how I came to work here. And I asked her how she came to work here. It's strange because there was a very long walk back from the gardens to the library, but no sooner had we started talking about life before Capmeadow than we were back here, on the museum tiles, saying goodbye and shaking hands.

When I got back to my chalet later that evening, I called Amber on her landline.

'It's me,' I said.

'It's the middle of the night,' said Amber's voice. It was really nice the way it sounded through the phone. Those phones have this very whispery quality to them. Her voice seemed to have a physical presence in the room, like an animal with soft hair, with teeth that fuzzed up her words.

'I was wondering if you would like to go for a walk,' I found myself saying.

'We went for a walk earlier,' she said. Then I could hear her breathing, I could picture her sitting up in her bed. I heard her drinking water. She had not said no.

'I know a place we can go,' I said.

'It's dark.'

'There's the moon. And the ambient lighting matrix, which allows the stars and moonlight in without any pollution of any kind.'

I heard her smile then. 'I like the way you talk,' she said.

'Very few people know about the floating market,' I said. 'But we could go now if you hurry.'

I really didn't know what I was saying. The idea of a floating market was just coming to me as I spoke, and yet I knew I was not lying.

'The floating market?'

'Sometimes, in the middle of the night, there is a market on the far side of Capmeadow Lake Number Two.'

I could hear the sound of her thinking again. A buzz in the phone.

'But why?' she said after a while. More awake now, but still not convinced. 'Who goes to a market in the middle of the night?'

I had the answer ready, even though I did not really know the answer at all.

'Certain things,' I said, 'cannot be made within Capmeadow. Certain produce must come from outside. This market is how these items have traditionally arrived. The floating market is an important moment in Capmeadow time.'

She laughed and I asked why she was laughing.

'You talk like nothing is real,' she said. I could not tell if there was still a laugh in her voice.

'I'm sorry,' I said. 'I didn't realise that was how I talked.'

I didn't exactly like hearing stuff like this from Amber. I found myself worrying in the silence.

'I was kidding, dumb ass!' she said and I was floating. 'I love the way you talk.'

'I love the way you talk, too.'

'OK, so where are we going then? How do we access this floating market?'

'I'll come and meet you,' I said. 'We can walk there!'

I put on soft clothes, they were from the loungewear range in the boutique on Little Alley in one of the newer areas of my district. They were meant to be worn after exercise or just for a stay-home day, but I felt they would suit the night air perfectly.

Out in the open, I felt strong and quick on my feet. I half walked, half ran to the building where Amber lived. The air seemed to give me energy. Something about the lights in these residential areas gives me a buzz. The grass was like green crystal, it didn't move at all. The air was so clean I felt dizzy, blue and black, with halos around every star, and a crown on half the moon. I was out of breath a little and rushing from the dopamine when I saw Amber.

'Ahoy, Amber!'

She looked nervous, her hands tucked into her sleeves as she waved.

'Ahoy!' she whispered, filling the air with that crackle in her voice.

My skin was hot. I wondered if I looked red. My face goes so red.

'It's this way,' I said. I was next to her. I could see my breath, and hers more delicate because she had not been running. Soon we were walking towards the second lake. This represented a more permanent boundary in the estate.

'I've never been this way, where are we?' Amber said after a while. We were reaching one of the early parking areas, from the days when they were used for cars. Now they housed vertical farms, salad parks, orchards, a pen of geese and chickens that were kept because they love eating slugs and sometimes would lay beautiful mineral-rich eggs. I know all this without knowing how. Do you know how I know all this? Did you teach me?

I didn't answer Amber, it seemed not to need a response. I kept looking at her though, and she was smiling. We were walking very fast, I realised.

We held hands again as we passed into the wetlands. Fog blew around us. Curled and blessed us. The light faded into the mist, it glowed like paint. Amber's eyes were wet, we covered our faces, but this was not the same as the mist inside the main estate, where buildings go up, this was older. From a time of no buildings.

'Talk to me,' Amber said. 'I can't see you.'

I started speaking without realising what I was saying, I felt like a guide. I have maybe always had this feeling.

'This land here was once countryside; long ago, water crept in to form marshes, peat soil bubbled here. I remember walking with my family. I remember my family. I was very small. It may not have been this land, it could have been anywhere, but I remember the ground beneath me going soft, rolling like a sadness.'

I do not know where the words were coming from, they appeared as I spoke. My skin itched wonderfully from the salt in my sweat.

'Keep talking,' Amber said.

'I walked too far ahead of my family, I heard them calling me, but I was pushing forward. I remember all of it as feelings but I can see the landscape, I can see it like something shattered. My nose was stuffed up and I could feel it swelling with blood. The pollen or something, blunting my nose, making my eyes run. Why are you doing this? That's what my parents were asking me. I didn't answer. I would never answer if I could avoid it. What could I say? I had no reason to give them, I just kept going. I was trying to get to the end, in a way, I was trying to finish first. I could hear my brother* behind me, he was calling too, his voice was insufferable to me on days like this, when he would line up with the parents, and not with me. I didn't know how to say, just catch up. I did not notice how wet my shoes were becoming. I noticed instead the broken bittiness of the land. Scratchy, and stinking. I looked for rats. I looked for mice and huge insects. I wanted to find the life that I could hear rustling, bubbling underneath all the bits. All the little hearts hammering. All the twigs and the grass. And more than anything I wanted to understand it, the way my family seemed to understand it. This whole area felt surely like broken space, like it needed to be cleared away, or it needed at least not to be disturbed by us. I was distracted by the business of it all, overwhelmed by it. At least the sky was clear, but in the sky, I saw hawks. Falcons. Tiny black dots, but strong, diving in and out.'

---

* **Archivist's note:** This brother feels poignant to me. I have tested the word inside here, in the archive itself, alone, I have tested the concept of a brother and I found it very difficult to continue. I saw the shape of a tall boy, the rough outline of hair, he is handing something down. The sensation made my chest hurt and I had to stop thinking about a brother in order to properly focus on my work.

'I grew up in the countryside,' Amber said. 'I've seen hawks. My grandmother would show me.' Her whispery voice again creaking and snapping in the air. It made my head shiver.

'Have you really?' I asked.

'I would watch these birds. Like the birds you're talking about. There were kestrels. They'd hunt the smaller birds. Sometimes I saw them bombing for robins who had strayed into the open. I saw one dead. Its small black eye looked at me like it was cursing me. What surprised me the most was how long it was when I picked it up by its feet. It was no longer a ball. But something long and thin, like a tiny sock.'

I thought about Amber carrying a dead bird. I could see her holding it up at arm's length and looking at it, seeing it swing. We didn't speak for a while.

Up ahead, the lighted marshland glowed. Lilac gels on the floor lamps cast shadows in the reeds. The light controlled everything. Over the other side of the lake, red and yellow lanterns glowed. The shapes of men and women on floating platforms, bugs diving at the water around our feet. I led Amber down to the lake beach. The huts that sold iced lattes and afterwork session IPA were boarded up, but still resonated calmness and safety.

We sat together and watched the movement across the lake. As I saw the dark, shadowy figures setting up their market stalls on floating platforms, the knowledge of what they were doing came to me.

'People come to trade their boutique projects and side hustles. These are the private initiatives of the Capmeadow population. You can see them, look.'

'I had no idea this existed.'

'It's surprising isn't it? But not new. We will soon be including this in the museum.'

We decided to go and take a look at what was happening. We had to walk a long way around the lake. We saw new paths forming a matrix of dramatic walkways. New forest land with repurposed vinyl tile routes through, and convenient aerated boulders appearing in the moonlight.

'This will make an excellent place to come on Sundays for casual time,' I said to Amber.

'Yes, casual time is wonderful near the water.'

We looked at the rocks.

'Do you think people will come here for sex?' she said.

The languid shapes on the surface of the rocks. 'Maybe. Yes.'

'These rocks look like they're made for it.'

Around us I became sure there were bodies. I could hear breathing. Moving and moaning in the growth. It was there for a moment and then gone.

'Shall we get closer?' I asked.

Amber stood up, ready to go. 'How do we cross?'

I led Amber to where I knew there would be a low pontoon at the water's edge. Thin wisps of fog curled up underneath the wood, and on the dark water circles appeared as small fish dibbed the surface. At the end of the pontoon was a small rowing boat with two oars. It looked like a rowing boat from a children's book.

'I know how to do this,' Amber said, and she climbed into the boat before me. It rocked and I gasped as I tried to find my seat. Amber laughed at me as I collapsed onto the little plank of wood. She began rowing, smiling, making a weird noise as she leant in towards me to dip the oars.

'When did you learn to do this?' I asked.

'I did a training session in the aquatics centre. It was just in the pool, but we all learnt how to row.'

I felt slightly ashamed and jealous because I had not visited the aquatics centre. I hadn't known about it. I didn't say anything for a while. It seemed ridiculous that I was upset about such a small issue. I knew about every restaurant, every shop, and of course my beloved museum, but I had no idea about the sports facilities here. I watched the oars dipping into the water, and felt hypnotised a little, and soothed. There was a kind of perfume in the mist, I realised, a fragrance coming from the floating market, where incense must have been burning.

'Do you remember your first day?' I asked Amber. I don't know why I asked her this. She looked at me coldly, a sort of warning.

'Of course I do,' she said. 'I was in training all day. I remember looking outside and wondering when the induction sessions would be done, so I could go and run on the track.'

'I remember the same thing,' I said. 'I remember the same feeling exactly, except that when I got out there, it was not a running track I wanted, but the team-gathering spaces and the retail/social zones. But I don't remember how I got here,' I said. 'I don't remember any of the journey, unless it was by train, but where would I have been coming from? I don't know. I don't know how I got here.'

'What a strange thing to say,' said Amber.

She actually glared at me this time, and then looked away. I didn't speak again. It felt like the crossing to the floating market was taking forever. I felt drowsier and drowsier and was about to fall into a really lovely sleep when the boat abruptly scooped round to the right. Amber had jammed one oar into the water, making us spin to a stop.

When she spoke, it was a harsh whisper. 'We can't talk about that stuff,' she said. 'Last time you talked to me about that, I woke up the next day with an awful awful headache. Please don't ask this stuff.'

'But I was just making conversation,' I said. 'It's no big deal. I have these long passages of my life where I remember it all, but only if I try not to look directly at it. I went to university in a sweet little town, and I had several bad hangovers, but mostly I read books and we cooked meals together in our house, and there were some financial hardships, some romantic horrors, but if I try to be specific, if I try to see the face of the person I was going out with, it just dissolves. And so I wanted to know if you also were like this. Not because I wanted to hurt you, or make you scared (because you seem so scared), but because it would mean I'm not alone. And it would mean that you are not alone, if you also had this condition, this sideways condition, where you cannot look too directly at your life, because if you do, the whole thing dissolves.'

Amber grabbed both of my hands and squeezed them. She looked at me in a way that felt at once horribly intense and violently tender.

'Do you remember the room I liked the most in the museum?'

'Yes. Wait. I think so?' I don't think I did remember.

'Go back to that room and take a look at the board. The pinboard.'

I had no idea what she was talking about. Her favourite room had been the long hall, I was sure, with the shapes that were forming. There was no board. I liked this room best too, and visitors seemed to enjoy it, although of course, as always, some of them were angry in that room.

There had been another place, a sort of junk room, where she had said, oh this is my favourite place, but she had been joking. She had tripped over a bucket. There was a pinboard in there. I resolved to go back to that room as soon as I could.*

'Will you go and look?' she asked again.

'Yes, of course.'

'Good,' she said. And then her whole expression broke apart and became placid once more. She turned the boat so we were heading towards the lanterns, and we smoothly continued to the floating market. We arrived at a low pontoon. Amber let me put a hand on her shoulder as I climbed out of the boat, and then I pulled her up after me.

We were met at the entrance to the floating market by a colleague in a warm-looking fisherman's jumper. It was a very dark navy, I think, though in the lantern light, I found it difficult to tell. Waxed wool, or something like it. There were a couple of shops in the shopping mall where this could have been acquired, but I realised it could also have come from one of the market stalls.

'None of this should be happening,' said the man in the fisherman's jumper. He was grinning and sweating.

'Sorry,' I said. 'It looks wonderful.'

The man in the knitted jumper hissed from the sides of his mouth. I could see from a quick glance around the stalls that several other people looked sweaty and angry in this way, but others looked happy and welcoming.

'Hello,' I said to the angry colleague. 'Do you need a glass of water?'

'No, thanks,' he said.

'Well, I hope things improve,' I said.

'I'm walking the dog.'

---

* **Archivist's note:** This pinboard is now in fact in the room where she receives people in her capacity as Liaison Officer.

'Hmm,' I said. 'I was wondering if that's waxed wool, your jumper?'

'I don't fucking know what it is,' he said.

Amber smiled but said nothing to him as she pulled me by the arm into the market. Our eyes met and we shook our heads. Amber is used to this kind of thing too, it seems. Or not used to it but aware of it. Familiar with some of the behaviour of people experiencing the expansion.

I bought a candle that was fragranced with fig and patchouli. And I bought some air-dried Palo Santo wood that you can burn and the smoke smells beautiful. It's used to cleanse the air, the colleague on the market stall told me.

'I normally work in product design,' he said. 'But me and my partner, Karen, we took an after-hours training session on perfume-making during employee appreciation week last year. Since then, we're obsessed with fragrances.'

'That's amazing,' I said. 'Where do you get your materials?'

'Ah, most of it comes from a perfume supply store in the old expansion of Middle Street. I think it's now called Baye Zone. Or it might have been absorbed into Dune Point.'

I nodded. I both knew exactly and had no idea what this place was. I was thirsty, and Amber bought me a spiced cider from the spiced cider stall. It was run by Anne Stone who works in Accounts Payable. She told me there was a place in the mall where she bought the sachets and the cider and the heated vat where she kept the cider just below boiling point.

'The idea just came to me in the night!' she said. 'I don't know if I'll be able to give up the day job, but I am passionate about this.'

It was delicious spiced cider. Then Anne Stone said, 'I have reported this whole place to the police. It's being investigated. They're going to come and tear it all down!'

When I asked her if she wanted a glass of water, she just laughed and took a big gulp of cider.

I joined Amber by the water's edge, where some crocheted bean bags had been laid out on a woven seagrass carpet.

'Things feel strange tonight,' Amber said.

'I'm still having a wonderful time,' I said. We held hands. I felt a memory come to me of my father waking me in the middle of the night, shaking me awake and telling me to get dressed. He was smiling the entire time, but he told me to hurry like I was late for something. It was dark outside. When I got downstairs, I found my brother and my mother also there, also dressed. Several suitcases were packed.

'Emergency holiday,' my father said.

'We're going to Disneyland for your birthday,' my brother* said.

I remembered it all exactly, every detail, and yet not one of the members of my family had a face.

Fog rolled in from across the lake; it seemed mixed with smoke. I felt suddenly engulfed. I held on tightly to Amber's hand. We did not move. The lights from the lanterns looked like embers loose in the mist. I felt the acrid perfumed smoke of Palo Santo drying out the inside of my throat. I felt my lungs burn. I heard screaming and splashing. I saw a shape in the mist, and a man was standing there. He was appallingly dressed.

'I think we should leave,' he said. 'This is not a safe place to be.'

It was a ludicrous thing to say, of course. There are multiple safety procedures that would obviously have rectified any momentary problem. We simply had to follow the fire safety

---

* **Archivist's note:** A sharp, wounding thought again of this brother. My job is difficult in these moments. If this even is my job.

procedure. But the man in dreadful clothes was holding out his hand to me with such a concerned look on his face that I decided to just go along with it. And yes, the floating market may also have been somewhat engulfed in flames. And there was a certain amount of screaming.

'We have a boat,' I said. 'Come with us.'

'There's only room for you though. Nobody else,' Amber said. I could tell that she did not want this man to come with us. He was indeed very heavy as a presence. He said his name was Tim or Tom* or something.

In the boat, sitting low in the dark water, we let Amber have the oars. She heaved while the man sat there with a completely expressionless face, half hidden by the shadows from the fire. He smiled at me very sadly when I asked him if everything was all right. It must have been a surprise that such an interesting event was taking place and so many new challenges were making themselves known to us. It must have been a shock, because he didn't seem able to speak. He kept *nearly* speaking, but then stopping himself. Very heavy.

This will sound very silly, and it must simply have been the mist or the fumes from the fire, but I noticed that I was crying a great deal as I looked at the man's sad face. His gristly little beard, his wonky lips. A huge pain exploded in my heart somewhere, as though far too much blood was entering and blasting out. I'm sorry for continuing to mention it, but yes, my whole chest felt like an iron cage. I felt as though something irreplaceable had been taken away from me, a combined surge of rage and heartbreak. But this feeling was coming from him, that's what has since become clear. This was something he was feeling and I was just picking up. And then my feet were wet

---

* **Archivist's note:** Yes, Tom Crowley. I confirm.

from wading to the lake shore. Both Amber and the man faded away into the night, in silence.

When I woke up this morning, I went back to the place where the floating market had been. There was nothing – no floating pads, no lanterns. Only black water textured by the lightest of breezes. That gorgeous sense of calm and the faint hint of incense on the air. I was struck again by the powerful thought that the Capmeadow expansion project never stops being a source of interest, challenge and innovation.

Before I came here, just before I came here to talk to you, I saw him again. The man who wore bad clothes. He sat down, like the others all do, and he began talking. He talked and talked.

While he was talking to me I became overwhelmed by something, I think it was him. I think it's him, he is so large, I feel like it's hard to breathe in the room with him, and yet, something about him makes me feel safe, and understood, or at least, I feel as though I once was safe, and once was understood. But he was also, somehow, he was also wrong. He was so wrong about something fundamental. I couldn't bear the weight of it. This has never happened to me before. I have been tired out – so exhausted – by the people who come and talk to me, but in a purely collegiate way. As a trusted partner in our work, I am considered OK to take some of their emotional load. We are all more effective when the load is shared. But this man was not sharing, he was reaching. His whole presence was so heavy, so weighing on me. I found it hard to breathe. I explained that he was mistaken.

I excused myself and came here. I feel a huge sense of imbalance. I feel that ragged – do you remember? – sense of detachment that I have sometimes tried to explain to you. Do you think it would be possible, if just for a moment, for me to have that thing, if I could just sit with it, and maybe brush its fur a little bit? I will be careful, I realise it is very old, and must not be allowed to leave this space. I feel like I know its name, but of course I don't. A little whistle sound.

Transcripts of footage from the archive #4: The fire

1. The floating market on the lake. Everything is lit with candles and lanterns. People smile from their stands, but their smiles look somehow dog-faced. Teeth show. In the dark, there are figures with their faces covered. Tom Crowley is there, he is looking at children's toys, he seems to be in a dream. As usual he is muttering to himself. He flinches when people go by. Zooming out, he is barely noticeable, it's just an ordinary professional scene of colleagues relaxing and unwinding in one of the many enrichment activities provided by the Capmeadow expansion experience. The fire starts out of the picture, but spreads rapidly. Tom rushes towards the water. He sees the Liaison Officer – something about the way she looks stops him in his tracks. He keeps blinking. It's as though he is noticing what I have seen all along, on screen at least:

    She is one of a number of people who seem more vivid within Capmeadow, whose smiles do not shake in the same way as others, who do not collapse in the middle of the walkway and have to be slowly doubted away from the archive.

Tom Crowley hears voices behind him. Voices of rage and violence. He has not long ago been attacked. The signs of it are on his face. He doesn't look sure at first if Amber and the Liaison Officer really do want him to join them in the boat. There is a moment when they stand and look at each other, the two women and Tom Crowley. The flames intensify, as though some new fuel has been licked by the fire.

The trio blindly scramble onto the boat.

The burning market is a vision of Hell. The sky seems torn with red smoke. Mist rolls in, extinguishing the flames. The little boat drifts away; those aboard seem barely conscious.

2. Presumably sometime later. Tom Crowley is in the museum, he is looking at the objects. He has a sad sort of smile. There are faded marks on him that could be burns. He does not look healthy, and yet he has that smile on him. He moves through the spaces of the museum. He looks from camera to camera, from sign to sign. The signs, even in the museum, cannot be seen correctly. I wonder again if this museum is just upstairs from the archive where I am sitting.

2. Tom Crowley arrives at the waiting area outside the interview room where the Liaison Officer (also known as **A voice** in this archive) conducts her meetings.

3. Inside the office of the Liaison Officer. Tom Crowley is looking at her. He looks ready to burst with what he

needs to say, and after every few breaths he tries to calm himself down. Behind where the Liaison Officer sits is a board. (I believe it is a pinboard, I remember them as a child, in my school, you would hand in your artwork to a teacher and they would pin it on the board. A pinboard. It's something I remember clearly, though I have not seen one in real life for a long time.) On the pinboard are many photographs. In one photograph, there are three children's faces. All girls. One of them has dark black and blue hair. The other two are similar-looking to one another. They are smiling and wearing giant fake spectacles. They are wearing badges that say, 'I went to work at Capmeadow!' One of the girls is holding a stuffed toy. It looks like a cat with a unicorn horn. Tom is transfixed by the image. I am transfixed by the image. One of the girls in the picture looks exactly like a girl would look if she was Tom Crowley's daughter. And in a way,* she looks like the Liaison Officer – who listens to Tom talking, talking and talking, and working himself up, and he's so happy to have found her.

But as he talks, and as she listens, you can tell she is feeling increasingly under the weight of him and his long, long story. I wonder if I see him flicker, I wonder if his eyes move away from her. I wonder if there is someone else who could be in that picture. I see a shape, a darker shape than the other girls, holding her own stuffed toy. And it has been so many years since I saw myself in a true mirror. The mirror here reflects darkly. It has been a long time since I saw myself. It must have been years. I do not know how long. Tom Crowley looks directly at

---

* **Archivist's note:** But only *in a way*.

the picture of me, through a camera in the room in the library. He smiles and something opens up in me, though this cannot be seen in the footage, but I am aware of how dark it is here, aware of all my nerves, and how afraid I am of being lost and left alone.

Transcribed footage #5: The outer limits

1. The outer limits of the Capmeadow park expand into a bright green desert. The ground is like glass, millions of tiny pale bottle-glass tiles. In the distance rises a vast temple. Alone, walking slowly, but with purpose, is the Liaison Officer (often referred to in this archive as **A voice**). The sun and the blue sky oppress her as she makes her way. After many hours, she reaches the vast double doors of the temple. They tower above her. She looks like a toy. The doors themselves, like the rest of the building, are made from a hardened, unashamed form of the pure matter that has built the expansion project into what it has become. The temple is called the Capmeadow Temple of Solitude, designated by an official Capmeadow building label. The outer walls of the building are carved with reliefs – scenes of work, meetings, workshopping sessions, hands clasped in celebration of collaborative working practices, and in a distant nook on the western wall of the oblong structure, there is an image of a worker being helped to her feet by those around her. There is an image of a happy child. There are shapes without faces. Curves and contours that imply dynamism,

success, misery, despair, loneliness, and in its totality, the enormous structure represents nothing more than it represents absolute loneliness. The Liaison Officer pushes open a small door within the largest main door, she goes inside. Watching, from within the wilderness of glass, Tom Crowley quietly pleads for her to wait, to listen. Tom Crowley turns and looks up at the sky, as if he sees the shapes of birds then sees the cameras looking down at him. I wave at him, and I try to speak, but my voice is broken. I try to say something to him but it is very heavy and impossible. He smiles a tiny bit, as though it's funny, as though it was all OK, and expected.

2. Inside the Temple of Solitude, the Liaison Officer finds a place to sit, and begins to talk. I do not watch her again. I have already transcribed what she says.

3. In the wilderness outside, dust flickers over the green glass desert; the Capmeadow Business Park continues to succeed and groan under the sound of its expansion – from here, the sound is more audible than ever, the sound of rubber and glass slowly moving, like an exit interview, like a frozen wave.

The archivist speaks

I think it's time I said something now. It was a wet day when I
came here. I believe it was a wet day – because I was soaking
wet. My clothes, my T-shirt, my – uh – the thing I was holding.
All soaked. There were pines already, growing in the far corners of the park. There were hellebores. I could smell pine the
whole time. I was holding someone's hand. It never felt like a
strange thing to think about until now – I remember their hand
but not the person. It was a man's hand, dry. The man I was
holding hands with did not use moisturiser. I was shown around
the borders of the park. I was given an abode. I remember but I
don't remember. I was assigned a buddy. I went to the canteen
with my buddy. My buddy explained to me that I would be
responsible for the archive, and took me down to the coolers
level. It took a long time to get down here.

I was holding something, I remember, and it would not be
taken away from me – it was not worth anyone's trouble, I
remember, trying to take that thing away from me.

This is your office, my buddy said. It's not easy to remember
what my buddy looked like, I feel like he was about my age,
and with a head like a small onion, a kind face really, with only
a minimal amount of hair on top of his head, not like balding,

but like the purple colouring at the top of a turnip, in pictures of turnips that I have seen, my buddy's head looked like that. There are so many people, aren't there, who come and go. It seems that way, though of course, I am alone here.

Perhaps it was him, this onion head that held my hand? I doubt it. Things seem strange now – when I try to remember the person who held my hand specifically, they seem to slip away.

My office is more like the bridge of a spaceship than an office. I have a large window that surrounds my seat and desk. The office is suspended, so through the windows, which lean outwards so I can look down, I see below me the vast cooling halls of the data centre. A darkness punctuated by the blinking lights of the data stations which are suspended in the rock above me. It goes out a way into the distance like a vast placid sea. There are no other rooms like mine. Nobody else is dangling down here. It's just suspended data and lights flickering in the darkness, and me.

The dark liquid down below my window, over which I am suspended, is the coolant. It is just a liquid, I was told. Was I told this? If you were to run your hand through it, it would be like cool water. It's only because the place is so dark that it looks black. Or maybe you couldn't run your fingers through it. Maybe that would be a terrible idea.

I have this idea – it's like a sub-idea (like the shadow of an idea, often representing the idea exactly contrary to the information you have been given as a fact, it hovers there, testing itself. The shadow idea says, This is not true. It says, What you are saying and what I am saying I believe, is not the truth. Does anyone else do this? Do you, the person in the archive who is reading this, even if you are me, do you do this?) – that it might drain memory from you, or move your memories around and reorder the data, this water. I have this idea that the liquid itself contains all of the data required to constantly expand the Capmeadow estate. You should never put your hand in the water. He wrote a sign to say this, I'm sure. He won't even have noticed that he did it. Don't put your hand in the water, I'm sure I've seen it. But certainty fades. I think the coolant contains organic data, and that's why you can't touch it.

I do not know what would happen if I drank the liquid, though I often think about it.

The lights pulse. The intensity of these lights comes and goes. Just now, a small and then a great surge. I imagine this is when a huge gulp of data is taken in, and the larger pulse is like a swallow.

I try to ingest the data of the archive that surrounds me. I try to structure my own memories, but the lights make me feel inadequate to the task of order. My own pulsing memory banks, formless and introverted compared to the ordered spectacle of the lights out there. In many ways, I am more sophisticated, but I'm also very inefficient and not valuable to the collective as a source of stored data. I have a memory, for example, of holding hands with an adult and being led down here to this work.

I remember seeing someone else holding hands with their adult. I came here as a child then, a visit, it must have been. I remember being shown the maps of Capmeadow. I have seen several historical pictures of the early expansion project. Although, early is a very difficult concept. Especially when I'm this tired.

I am so tired.

I have plenty of breaks, and there is a relaxation area within my room. I go there often – just now I was there – I can sit and relax. Or I can play video footage from around Capmeadow.

Anytime I like, I can look at any particular place, a particular moment in the evolution of the site.

I can see the man who is wearing shabby, somehow permanently creased clothes whose name is Tom Crowley. The controls are strange, I suppose. Not how I was told it would be in my training, which was completed online before I arrived for my first day of work. I use these interfaces, it's hard to explain them. There's one that feels like a grandmother's face. It's like a trackpad, but has feeling. Also, things are not organized by date, but by development phase of the expansion project. Things are not organized at all, as far as I can see. The archive swells around me. At night, if it is night, I can hear it groaning and breathing. I have a few things with me. There is a toy here, a stuffed toy, that I keep losing and then finding. It is very ancient, it seems to me. I believe it has some relevance to the things I am detailing here. I yearn for it. I lose it and yearn for it and then I find it again.

'We don't know what to do with that,' my line manager told me. She was only here for a while. I haven't heard from her in a long time. She has never attended any of our scheduled meetings. I know what to do with it, this stuffed toy. A child's toy. You can buy similar items in the lower mall. There is a shop that sells toys, craft ideas and other treats. I never see children in Capmeadow, apart from Bring Your Daughter to Work Day. But presumably parents must work here.

'I'm holding my son, who is devastated,' someone might say. A simple statement of the kind we hear all the time, and which slips in and out of the archive. These comments are not forbidden in themselves, but certainly the audio record of it being said, if there is an audio record of it being said, is obscured and weakened. Eventually it has gone from the memory. The video records do not show clearly the movement of mouths. I've tried to see! You can zoom all the way into – actually to the inside of – a mouth if you freeze the frame while someone is yawning or shouting. If you cut in while they talk, it blurs, the lips twist on themselves. The face becomes monstered. I see it sometimes when I lose track of myself, the twisted reconstituted mouths.

This is problematic because as an archivist, I expect to see some linear consistency, something I can cling to, and link together in a way that makes sense. Or that might make sense once a few roads have been followed. But here, things become difficult because the expansion project development phases have undergone many new naming conventions. Which would be fine, except it's not actually clear which naming convention came first. Expansion phases have been referred to by some colleagues in the archives as 'formerly known as', and yet, when I check for audio captures of the formerly known term, the new term is referred to as 'formerly known as'. Around the breakout area there are several piles of paper notebooks in which I have tried to piece together a linear time sequence that explains the expansion of the business park in days and weeks and months and years and decades and so on.

I had to stop with this project. The breakout area became depressing to me. I slept amongst these works many times. It was a relief when I woke up at some point maybe a month ago and saw the door of my office closing and the vanishing shape of a colleague from the estates team, and heard the quiet dragging of a bin bag out in the corridor. They had come in and taken away all of my notes. I have not committed anything to paper since then. Only this record in the margins of the true archive. I suppose eventually this too will be removed – though not by the bin-liner method. Soon everything I have recorded here will be cut – sucked out into one of those lights, and lost in the black coolant.

These days, when I relax in the breakout area, my mind drifts back to her. The woman in the interviews. The Liaison Officer. The one who fell in love with the museum – with the idea that such a thing could magically exist – I think of her and dream about her life. I try to imagine her going to the 'beach' at the edge of the silent lake. I have seen footage of her going there many times. She walks with such confidence through the landscape, but every now and again, she looks around. She seems to be looking for someone. She seems to suddenly lose confidence in what she's doing. She looks lost, and then she shakes her head and continues on her journey.

At the beach, she unrolls a towel and lies down, lets the sun warm her. The breeze ripples the water and she covers herself with a light blanket she has brought for this exact purpose.

I pause, search through the archive to find the moment that she bought the blanket. She is in one of the shops that opened in the precinct, traded for a few days, and then was repurposed into something else. She pays entirely with Capmeadow credit. She is fully committed to life here.

She intersects with so many of the anomalies in the records. That was how I first discovered her. She was so quiet compared to the others. She was not raving.

It is thrilling to think that this room might be just a few floors below where she sits in the museum. Her presence in this building has been my archival obsession since I realised nobody is really paying attention to my work. I remember her.

Final transcript in this section of the archive

4. In the NuYu tropical peace gardens. Mist crawls around
   the floor. The water in the carp pond is dark black. Three
   girls, they must be around eight years old, dare each
   other to get closer to the water. The bodies of fish in
   the water shock and amuse them. The fish look like dis-
   membered arms, living and grasping at each other. The
   girls dare each other to touch the water. On three they
   plunge their hands in. There is a flash. The three of them
   look towards the source of the light, their faces frozen
   in shock. The mist rises. The screen whites out. Nothing
   else can be seen. I am not supposed to have access to this
   footage. Several lights in the room where I am looking at
   this footage are flickering horribly. I cannot scroll back.
   The archive is forgetting them. I cannot get back to
   them. But I can try – if there is time. Maybe there will
   be time.

5. The archivist, an ageless, defeated shape, sits hunched
   inside the small archive office, suspended above the
   black lake, surrounded by the winking lights of a million
   servers. She rises and with her hands takes up her heavy
   metal chair. She begins, in slow splinters, to shatter the

glass window. She climbs onto the ledge. She takes a final look around, and continues to dive into the water below.

In the darkness, we grow, we succeed together, we love and break together. I am so sorry I ran away.

Acknowledgements

SENIOR LEADERSHIP ANNOUNCEMENTS

I am so grateful to my editor, Jason Arthur, to my agent, Cathryn Summerhayes, to Sigrid Rausing and to everyone at Granta and Curtis Brown who has worked on this book.

MILESTONES AND ACHIEVEMENT AWARDS

I'll never be able to repay the generosity, time and encouragement given by Tim MacGabhann, Charlie Tittle, Claire Caroll, Tom Connaghan, Luke Kennard, Naomi Wood, Jack Underwood, Kevin Riddle, Charlie Turnbull.

Special thanks to everyone who has dropped a kind word my way over the years after reading a story.

RECOGNITION WALL: HUMAN STORIES OF THE YEAR

Thanks to Luke Neima for the now legendary pizza chat of old/new Finsbury Park. Thanks to Nick Blake, who has helped my writing more than I've so far been able to express.

PROMOTING OUR VALUES AROUND THE WORLD

Deepest gratitude and love to all my family (plus extenders) – especially Tom Pester (who let me use his name as long as the character would be 'wounded in some way'), Holly Pester, Liz Waugh (my wonderful mum), Uncle Kit, my dad, Bryn Tittle, Emma Bennett, Killian Fox and Rod Colman.

Thank you Emilie, Coco and Orson – God only knows what I'd be without you all.

TO ALL OUR COLLEAGUES

Sincere thanks to all of Fun Club, including Nick the Snick, Ruth Cosgrave and Patrisha Townsend Green.

And finally, to everyone I have ever worked with – in offices, supermarkets, airports, call centres, pubs, restaurants, theatres and cinemas – and will work with again tomorrow, thank you for sticking with me. This book is really for you.